AND THE WIND BLOWS FREE

Also by Luke Short

in Thorndike Large Print

Ride the Man Down

The Guns of Hanging Lake

Play a Lone Hand

Ramrod

AND THE WIND BLOWS FREE

by

Luke Short

Thorndike Press • Thorndike, Maine

Library of Congress Cataloging in Publication Data:

Short, Luke, 1908-1975.
  And the wind blows free / by Luke Short. --
  [Large print ed.]
  p.   cm.
  Reprint. Originally published: New York : Bantam Books,
  1945.
  ISBN 0-89621-869-4 (alk. paper : lg. print)
  1. Large type books. I. Title.
[PS3513.L68158A85   1989]   89-4414
813'.54--dc19   CIP

Large Print edition available by arrangement with
H. N. Swanson, Inc. Agency.

Cover design by James B. Murray.

Yes, we buried him there on the
   lone prairie

Where the owl all night hoots mourn-
   fully;

And the blizzard beats and the wind
   blows free

O'er his lonely grave on the lone
   prairie.

"THE DYING COWBOY"

One

I was eighteen in that year, 1884, and Jim Wade was thirty. This is his story, as much of it as I know, and knowing only this much I think of him kindly.

That was the year the trail herds, as never before, were rolling up from Texas on the Chisholm trail through the Indian Territory to railheads like Caldwell, Kansas, more than a million head of longhorns in a summer. That was the year ugly rumors came with them, rumors that at last the Cheyenne and Arapaho were threatening revolt against a government that was starving them, and were raiding the passing trail herds for food.

That was the year when cattlemen in the peaceful Cherokee Outlet that lay below Kansas looked enviously south to the deep grass of the Indian Territory and said: "We need the grass, but all hell will break loose down there. No thanks."

And that was the year Jim Wade, in the face

of this growing trouble, leased another million acres of wild and desolate grasslands from the Cheyenne chiefs and sent up to Caldwell for enough wire to run in four strands for two hundred and forty miles through the heart of the Cheyenne and Arapaho reservation.

That was Jim Wade. He fought a little harder, got a little more than his fellows, climbed a little higher – sometimes on the necks of less determined men – and fell a little further in the end, but he was a man with an idea and I was part of that idea.

I think I was the only person in Caldwell who had not seen Jim Wade, and that was strange considering that I was the lone clerk in the two-room office of Tressel, Satterfield and Wade, Drovers. It wasn't strange, however, if you knew my employers. The July day I got off the stifling train at Caldwell, Kansas, and fought my way through the rough and drunken and profane crowd to the office above the Caldwell *Free Press*, I found only an itinerant sign painter engaged in painting the firm's name on the glass of the door. Nobody was in the office; nobody showed up there for two days.

On the third day Mr. Tressel, my father's old friend from Texas and the firm's member with whom I had corresponded, found me at the Drover's House and showed his kindness to be more eloquent than any apology. Mr. Satterfield, a shy little New Englander, I saw once in the first month before he went East. But Jim Wade I did not see. He was only a word on the door, not even a signature on a letter.

And it was eight months before I did see him. In that time I had learned my job, which dealt strictly with the sale and shipping of trail herds, and liked it. I had got over being homesick for St. Louis and had met a girl, Elizabeth Lowell, distantly related to the Boston Lowells, whom I secretly wanted to marry when she completed her schooling in the East. The fall shipping was done and the last of those uproarious nights was past when the Texas cowboys were saying goodbye to a trail town until another summer. The prairie had turned brown and the fall rains rolled in under low skies to find the big stock pens empty, and the snows had locked the rutted streets of Caldwell into ridged and dirty ice scoured clean by the winds. But Jim Wade was still only a name that Mr. Tressel did not discuss with me, but which I heard mentioned time and again in hotels, in the post office, in the barber shops and in the saloons. Because I was an employee of his and not yet over a certain shyness, I would even defend him in amiable argument without knowing anything about him except what I had picked up in another argument the evening before. This one thing I did learn and still know: men were never indifferent to him.

With the coming of February Mr. Tressel seemed to forget me for a drover does not do business in winter and Mr. Tressel abominated towns. While he was at our firm's small holdings in the Cherokee Outlet to the south of Caldwell, I was alone and with nothing to do except pay my nightly calls on Elizabeth, who had stayed home from her school in the East this winter to favor a weak chest. Fearing that Mr. Tressel was too kindhearted to pay me off in a slick shipping season I resolved to improve my time some way, and I borrowed law books to study during those slack daylight hours.

I was so engaged one morning, my feet turned toward the small stove to compound the comfort the deep leather easy chair was giving me, when I heard steps on the outside stairs. They were too agile to be Mr. Tressel's, even though it was a blustery day; but I did not want to get the reputation around town of being an idler, so I shut my book, sought my high stool and opened a ledger.

The man who stepped into the hall was wearing a buffalo-skin coat, and when he opened it against the heat of the room I saw that his dress was in no way different from the cowboys of the Cherokee Outlet, who now made only our Saturday nights a torment. He wore corduroy trousers tucked into the tops of high-heeled knee boots, a brown flannel shirt and a silk neckerchief wound tightly around his throat, the knot at the side.

"Mornin'," he said — only the word was a cross between "Mawnin'" and "Moanin'" to my ears. It wasn't the way a Negro would say it and it wasn't the way our Mississippi Riverboat captains in St. Louis would say it.

He received my greeting with a courteous nod and then glanced carefully about the room. I thought I saw a smile start on his browned face, but it never came off. He was a tall man, thick at the chest, and he was clean-shaven, which was rather unusual for those times. The wind had driven color into his face at the high cheekbones, and I noticed the skin at the corner of his gray eyes was wind-puckered, leathery. I never did know what it was that gave his face in conversation a look of veiled and skeptical impudence that was wholly friendly. It held invariable respect, but you could tell that the respect stemmed from manners and good will, not from subservience or inferiority. His high thin nose was twisted a little at the bridge, and the cold had whitened a tiny scar there. At first I thought the black hair at his temples was gray-shot, but it was powdered with snow.

He tramped across the room and opened the

door into what had been the law library of the former tenant. It was vacant, but he took the trouble to look even behind the door.

"Your partner here, Mr. Wade?" he asked, turning to me.

"I'm not Mr. Wade," I said. "Which partner do you want to see?"

"I've been told Mr. Satterfield isn't here. I want that scoundrel Tressel."

I don't know which came first, surprise or anger. I stared at him, but he coolly stared me down and I felt my face getting hot, and I said angrily, "Mr. Tressel isn't here. Besides, he's no scoundrel and you wouldn't dare call him that to his face!"

"It's fortunate he isn't, I reckon," he drawled, still staring at me. "I would hate to pistol whip a cow thief in his own office, Mr. Wade."

"I'm not Mr. Wade!" I cried. "And Mr. Tressel never stole a cow in his life!"

"I intend to hear him name me that lie, Mr. Wade, before I whip him." He nodded again and said, "Thank you kindly, and good day."

He started for the door. I called, "You're wrong! Mr. Tressel isn't a thief! You're making a mistake!" He didn't answer me, and went out, slamming the door in anger behind him.

I listened to him thunder down the stairs and take to the boardwalk, the snow creaking noisily as he passed under my window. When my heart stopped thumping and I was able to reason again, I judged that the man was either a liar or a troublemaker, but if either he could do harm.

And then I realized that Mr. Tressel had promised to be in town today. He seldom came first to the office, instead stopping in at the Drover's Bar for a warming drink and the news, and it was there that I must look for him and warn him. For in spite of his gray hair and his spare old body Mr. Tressel had a temper and had been known to thrash a town bully with his fists.

I leaped off the stool and grabbed my hat but not my coat and took the icy stairs two at a time. Looking up the street, I could not see the stranger. I ran then. Rounding the corner of the Drover's House, the wind funnelled under the wooden awning down the whole length of the street, tore at me, and my hat went sailing into the road. I did not stop, but ran on past the hotel to the saloon next door and wrenched open the storm doors and lunged inside.

The stranger and Mr. Tressel were drinking together at the bar. At my entrance, Mr. Tressel looked over his shoulder and called, "Shut the door, Joey, and come here. This is Jim Wade."

I know I looked a fool with my hair blown awry, hatless, out of breath and my hands red, a gangling, green young man who was the butt of a joke he was just beginning to understand. And I know there was murder in my eyes as I looked at Jim Wade. This was the middle-aged stockman, my employer, the man known and respected by every stockman and cowboy of the Kansas trail towns, this — this clown! Jim Wade's face was bland and innocent, and when Mr. Tressel put his hand on my shoulder saying, "Jim, this is Joel Hardy, our office boy," and Jim took my hand and murmured, "An honor, Mr. Hardy," I could have murdered him cheerfully. I believe I only looked surly and shamed.

Jim Wade turned to the bartender and said, "Ask Mr. Hardy's pleasure, George, and we'll have two more of the same." Later, I realized how considerate that was, for he gave me time to compose myself. He never did tell Mr. Tressel about our meeting in the office.

Such was my introduction to Jim Wade, and I believe the manner of it favored me, for dating from that day my relations with the firm were not so much those of an employee as of an equal. Jim Wade disappeared the night of the day we met. Two days later Mr. Tressel entered the office and he was carrying a small ledger.

"Joey, close the firm's books," he said, laying the ledger before me. "Open these new books under the name of Canadian Cattle Co., Incorporated. The first entry will be a check for seven thousand dollars deposited to the credit of Edmonds Brothers, Indian Traders, Fort Reno."

"Fort Reno, sir? In the Indian Territory?"

"Yes, sir. It's the garrison post for the Cheyenne and Arapaho. When you've got that done, clean out your inkwells, leave the key downstairs, deposit the check at the Stockman's Bank and pack up." He put a hand in his pocket and pulled out a purse. "Have you any debts unpaid? No? Good. You're takin' stage with me this noon for Indian Territory."

I am certain the dismay on my face was not wholly concealed from Mr. Tressel as he went out. Like every young man, I had heard stories of the Territory, that vast land which was later to become part of Oklahoma but which now served as permanent sanctuary for the Indian tribes. Only last week the *Free Press* had printed a story of two men found murdered in their buggy some sixteen miles from Fort Reno. They had been shot while sleeping, and the only plausible explanation was robbery by parties unknown. It was common knowledge that outlaws wanted in every Territory in the West were in hiding there under the sufferance of Indians only a little less murderous than themselves. And of all these Indians, the Cheyenne, sharing millions of acres of prairie in the west central part of the Territory with the

15

peaceful Arapahos, were the least predictable and the most savage. Small wonder I was more uneasy than excited as I prepared to abandon the office that morning.

When my business was done, I went downstreet to say goodbye to Mr. Lowell, Elizabeth's father, who owned an emporium for stockmen's outfittings. He seemed surprised and annoyed that I was leaving, and when I could tell him only where I was going and not when I would return he looked at me as if surely I were half-witted. From the store I hurried to Lowell's small white house upstreet to say goodbye to Elizabeth and her mother.

My news appalled them. We sat in the parlor a moment, and I exchanged gloomy stares with Elizabeth. Her small delicate face, always strikingly pallid against the dark dresses she favored, seemed to pale even more as she considered my announcement. Perhaps her thoughts were the same as mine. We liked each other, her family approved of me, and now I had a start at learning a business. Months from now, when she was more sure of me and I was more sure of my abilities, we could become engaged. In another year, I would marry her and take her out of sordid, frontier Caldwell, perhaps to St. Louis. How these plans were to fit in with my ambitions at law I hadn't considered.

Mrs. Lowell could have been thinking along the same lines when she said at last: "But you were hired as a drover's clerk, Joel, to work in Caldwell. I should certainly refuse to be moved."

"It's not fair, Joel," Elizabeth said sharply. I was touched by her anger, which I considered stemmed from her loyalty to me. "You won't even have an office."

"Probably not."

"Jim Wade has always been a high-handed man," Mrs. Lowell said. "No, Joel, I should certainly refuse."

But I knew I couldn't, because of my debt to Mr. Tressel. And I felt a faint boyish stirring of loyalty to Jim Wade, who certainly had not been high-handed with me. I said, "I guess I'll have to try it, Mrs. Lowell," and stood up. Mrs. Lowell bade me a worried and disapproving goodbye, and left me with Elizabeth.

I found it difficult to say the things to Elizabeth in daylight that I could say in darkness. We were too young, too uncertain of the future and too disappointed to even plan our next meeting. Our parting was unsatisfactory and awkward, made more so by my haste and by Elizabeth's reluctance to see me go.

I hustled back to the Drover's House in time to hand my thin valise to a taciturn and burly stage driver whose three coats and two scarves

17

made him look like a mobile beer barrel.

We left Caldwell in a six-place Concord stage, a piano tuner from Arkansas City our only companion. South of town we passed the tent and wagon settlement of the Boomers who, rumor had it, were planning another attempt to invade the Indian Territory for settlement in the spring. The persistence of these hoemen, land hungry and determined, to settle the Indian lands in the face of the army's strict orders to turn them back had won them the enmity of all the stockmen, and Mr. Tressel's remarks about them were anything but kindly.

I was impatient of the piano tuner's presence, because I wanted to ask Mr. Tressel questions about my new work and could not with this stranger in the seat across from us. Mr. Tressel wanted to talk too, I thought, but he only smoked a series of thin black cheroots and pointed out the holdings of the various ranches in the Cherokee Outlet as we passed south over its wintry range.

We put up at the Pond Creek stage station that night, and a more disagreeable night I never spent. At sundown, the cold bore down on the land like iron and stilled the wind. All through the early evening I watched the main room of the frame house fill up with cowboys, most of whom were line riders seeking shelter from the cold snap. Added to the four freighters, whose oxen were stalled in the out-buildings and whose freight wagons were ranked along the south side of the house out of the wind that did not blow, these riders brought the number of occupants in the house to thirteen. There was whiskey and, of course, poker, which Mr. Tressel joined. The piano tuner and I turned in on two hammocks slung in the passageway between the kitchen and the common room, as the beds were already taken by the stage driver, three freighters and a sick cowboy. I slept with Mr. Tressel's buffalo coat over me to kill the draft from broken windows.

Next morning the cold still held, and the piano tuner, a frail man and none too warmly dressed, decided to lay over for the day. The stage pulled out at sunup with only Mr. Tressel and myself as passengers. It was a bitter day and we huddled together for warmth in the lurching gloom of the stage whose canvas curtains were pulled down to keep out the weather. My job at Fort Reno, Mr. Tressel told me, was to post notices and receive bids for the cutting of fence posts, on which the Canadian Cattle Co. was going to string wires on three sides of its lease for the distance of one hundred and seventy miles. After he said that I waited for him to correct himself, for the figure was fantastic to me. When he did not, I looked over at him, but his seamed old face was screwed up in an effort to break the frost ice which was riming his full white mustache.

"How many acres is that, sir?" I asked.

"About two million and a half." He understood what I was thinking and he chuckled. "Big, eh, Joey? It would be bigger if Jim Wade had his way."

"But aren't these Indians hostile?"

"Jim Wade says no man is hostile to money, not even an Indian," Mr. Tressel said. It seemed that Jim Wade, while not the first to discover this fact, was the first to put the knowledge of it into effect on a grand scale. The barber-shop version of it I already had; it remained for Mr. Tressel to explain the bare and exciting fact.

During the last few years Texas had been called upon to stock the enormous ranges of the north – Wyoming, Montana, Colorado, Nebraska and Dakota – besides supplying the East with its meat. But if the thin-blooded Texas cattle were to withstand the rigorous northern winters without a huge loss, they must first be introduced to winter. This fact had put a premium on those grazing lands whose winter was a kind of purgatory between the south and the north. The big Cherokee Outlet south of the Kansas line was ideal and every foot of it was leased. But below the Outlet lay the vast ranges of the Cheyenne and Arapaho, with a similar winter, and its grass was belly high to a horse. In all this great land which had once been buffalo range, only a few scattered ranchers grazed their herds on sufferance of the Indians.

All the big cattlemen, desperate for range, had coveted this grass, but only Jim Wade had acted. He called together all the Cheyenne and Arapaho chiefs, who were hungry and hostile at a government which did not recognize that the buffalo were gone and that even Indians must eat. Jim proposed to lease a million acres of their range, to be paid for in beef or money or both, and his proposition was accepted.

And like all men of vision, Jim Wade was in for abuse. The host of army camp followers — the beef contractors, the freighters, the squatters on Indian land, the second-guessers and the envious — fought him bitterly. Above all else, the government itself could not make up its mind about him. The War Department warned him he could expect no protection from it against hostile Indian uprisings, or against rivals. He had even been scolded by Mr. Teller, the Secretary of the Interior, who told him in a letter which was later to become famous that his lease was not recognized as legal by the Department of the Interior; that he must take his chances on the good faith of the Indians, and that his lease might be terminated at any moment by the government.

Jim Wade, a man walking a tight-rope, laughed at that, Mr. Tressel said. His answer was to go East (on borrowed money, for he had run himself into debt by the payment of the first grass money to the Cheyenne and Arapahos) and obtain financial backing. Mr. Tressel said he returned to Texas with the money of an eastern Senator, a New York banker, a New England mill owner and a New York play producer. He had lost twenty pounds and he drank a water glass of whiskey before breakfast to steady drink-shot nerves. He had come out of it not only with the necessary backing but with a huge block of stock for himself and his old partners in the drover business, Mr. Tressel and Mr. Satterfield, and with absolute management of the company.

With the money to buy cattle and lease range, with the consent of the chiefs, all that remained for him to do was to occupy the range, and that was not easy, Mr. Tressel said. There were white men in the Nations who had made a business out of leasing Indian land to ranchers in payment for money, and they, in turn, would pay the Indians in cheap whiskey. All these men, the whiskey-peddlers, the squatters, the half-breeds, the malcontent Indians and the riffraff seeking sanctuary in the Nations, fought him. Jim got a crew of thirty men, and he had not been gentle, but he had won.

Right now, he intended to draw his boundary lines in wire, and it was my job, Mr. Tressel said, to help in that.

He himself was on his way to Texas by way of Fort Sill, in the Comanche territory south of the Cheyenne and Arapaho reservation. The additional cattle which would complete the stocking of our Cheyenne and Arapaho lease this coming summer would come from the Texas panhandle and the upper tier of Texas counties. That was where I was to join Mr. Tressel after my business was done and together we would assemble the herds. I was to be a bookkeeper for a drover's firm in summer, a buyer, bookkeeper and agent for a cattle company in winter.

I learned all this piecemeal on the four days our stage plunged deeper into the Indian country. Much of the time we followed the Chisholm trail, a great brown highway rutted inches deep that ribboned across the Indian territory. The millions of cattle that made it had tramped down the creek and river banks so that our stage had an approach to the fords. It was a wild and lonely land, locked in a winter whose snow at times almost smothered the grass. It sloped and tilted in brown and white hills, and then dived into the bottom lands grayed by the bare willow fringes and cotton-woods and blackjacks. We passed toiling freighters with their canopied wagons drawn by plodding oxen, and less often we saw single Indians on ponies. The plow had not touched this land, and the Cimarron was only a deep and lonely gash in the rolling prairie. The few cabins we saw were the poor shacks that were stage stations on the way to Fort Reno.

By the fifth day the desolation of it was depressing to me, for I was a person of towns. Here was nothing, only space and grass and low hills belonging to Indians who only ten years before had risen to massacre the white settlers to the north, and who were again threatening our people. As a red winter sun set that evening, touching the snow patches with pink before cold darkness rolled in from the east, I knew the full meaning of being a stranger in a strange land.

"A horse," Mr. Tressel said suddenly, "was born to carry, not to pull. Damn a stage, anyway."

That admission of discomfort consoled me somewhat, and I settled down in the dusk to listen to the rumble of wheels, loud and cheerless.

Moments later, the stage slackened speed and finally stopped and I unfastened the curtain and poked my head out to see what the trouble was. In the cold dusk I could see that two horsemen had stopped us. They switched over in front of the horses to Mr. Tressel's side and engaged our driver in conversation.

Presently, I heard the driver climb down and he opened the door on Mr. Tressel's side.

"Mr. Tressel," he drawled, "you feel like payin' these two men any money?"

Mr. Tressel said, "What's that?" and leaned over so he could see out. He muttered something and then he threw the robe from him and climbed out. I followed.

"Now, what's this, Harvey?" Mr. Tressel said, once he was on the ground.

"You feel like payin' them any money?" the driver repeated, gesturing to the two men who had now dismounted. They were both Indians, I could see, although there was a slight difference in their dress. One wore a blanket over his head and wrapped around him, and his rifle stuck out from between its folds. The other wore a hat and heavy duck jacket, and his cloth trousers were tucked into the tops of his Indian leggings. Twin braids hung down onto his lapels. He also held a rifle in his hands.

Mr. Tressel examined them closely and his stare was accepted by them in surly silence.

"Why?" he asked.

"They claim we're passin' over their land and that we should pay."

Mr. Tressel murmured softly, "They do, do they?" and took a step toward the two, but

Harvey laid a hand on his arm.

"My treat, Mr. Tressel," Harvey said, and walked up to the coated Indian and hit him in the face. There was more than the sound of flesh striking flesh; there was a tearing, slippery sound which I cannot describe, but when the man came to rest on his back in the snow, I understood what had happened. His nose, bleeding, was flat and mashed.

Harvey turned to the other Indian and spoke one quiet word in a language I did not understand. I was waiting for the Indian to shoot him, or hit him, but the Indian simply turned to his horse, mounted, and rode north, leaving his companion.

Mr. Tressel came up to the supine man and, regarding him, said quietly to Harvey, "That's a trick I didn't think you young fellows knew."

Harvey chuckled. "My old man learned me that. You bust an Indian in the nose just once and there ain't no fight."

"But he's not a full-blood, is he?"

"No sir, I don't reckon. He's a breed and that's why I picked him. If he was an Indian we'd of had a tussle on our hands. But them Cheyennes hate a breed as much as we do."

Mr. Tressel said. "That's lucky," and climbed back in the stage. Harvey climbed back to the driver's seat and I, without having said a word, climbed in after Mr. Tressel. If this sounds casual, I report it as it happened. As for myself, I had been only amazed.

Mr. Tressel lit a cheroot and presently observed with magnificent irrelevance, "A cigar is no smoke in the cold, Joey," and lapsed into silence.

He did not speak again until there was a noticeable gain in the speed of the stage, which indicated we were going down hill.

Mr. Tressel said, "Look out your curtain, Joey." I did and I saw a smear of lights below and far away. "That's the agency," he said. "Beyond it and across the river up there on the hill is Reno, and one of those lights is food and drink, I think."

The horses hoped so too, for minutes later we rolled through the main street of Darlington, the Cheyenne and Arapaho agency. The driver heaved a sack of mail onto the porch of the Murphy Hotel as we passed, shouted something to the man who picked it up, and we were again in darkness. We passed through the forest of the bottomlands, crossed the wide and almost waterless Canadian River with a scrabble of cracking ice, pulled slowly up the long bare hill and wheeled into the grounds of Fort Reno garrison. In the tradition of all stages, we took the stretch along the parade grounds at a gallop and pulled up at the huge square building of Edmonds Brothers Trading Post with a screech

27

of brakes and a wild skid.

Jim Wade was there on the porch, waiting for us. He jumped down and yanked open the stage door and looked at us and laughed. "Gentlemen, hush! Here comes misery in a pair."

Mr. Tressel climbed out, saying, "Jim, I don't even aim to be civil until I get a drink."

"There's hot water and likker in my room, sir. You and Joey get along and I'll rustle up your valises." He put out his hand to me and smiled and said, "How you been, boy? The magnolias in blossom up your way?"

I laughed and said they were not and Mr. Tressel paused on the porch, called, "Harvey, this is my treat now. Your score at the bar is on my bill tonight."

"Obliged, Mr. Tressel," Harvey said, grinning.

The hotel was on the second floor of Edmonds Brothers Trading Post, a great square building that contained a huge general store, the post office, two bars, and a barber shop, with a wagon yard and livery stable behind it. From the window of my room upstairs I could look down on the garrison buildings placed around the bare parade grounds, but could make out the details of none. There were street lamps flanking the parade grounds and one high building had lights in two stories. I do not know what I expected to find at Fort Reno, but after our five lonely and uncomfortable days on the stage, I was surprised to see gravel drives, stone walks and street lamps.

I washed and went to Jim's room and met Mr. Edmonds, who had a drink with us, and then we went into the dining room, which was deserted except for our party. Jim had warned the cook and our supper was ready. Jim sat across the table from us, pipe in mouth, and talked with us as we ate. He was dressed in a black suit tonight, with a pleated bosom white shirt and a loose black bow tie. His boots, with trouser ends still tucked in them, were polished dully, and I believe I never saw him make a greater concession than this to the dress of any society.

Mr. Tressel was lighting his after-dinner cigar when an army man entered the dining room. He was a second lieutenant, young, blond and trim-looking in his blue uniform, and he seemed to know Mr. Tressel, who greeted him warmly. His name was Tom Wynant, and after shaking hands with me and accepting a cigar from Mr. Tressel, he pulled up a chair and said, "The Major sends his compliments, Mr. Tressel, and says he waits your pleasure to prove that Nathan Forrest had more fight than brains."

Mr. Tressel fixed him with a friendly glare. "Does the Major know that if Nathan Forrest had commanded enough horses to mount his guerrillas, the war would have ended in sixty-four with Forrest's capture of Bangor, Maine?"

"The Major doubts that, sir. He says he has proof that Forrest thought the Atlantic Ocean formed the eastern boundary of Pennsylvania."

Mr. Tressel took his cigar from his mouth and leaned forward. "Nathan Forrest was an educated gentleman, sir. He —" Mr. Tressel paused and looked over at Jim, who was grinning with delight. A slow smile broke over Lieutenant Wynant's face and Mr. Tressel settled back in his chair, the skin at the corner of his eyes wrinkling in amusement. "I've a sound notion to thrash you for your insolence, Tom."

Lieutenant Wynant laughed easily. "And you could do it too, sir. No, my instructions were to invite you and Jim and Mr. Hardy to the hop and german at the Hall tonight. The Post is having a party for the agency folks and the Coes, who got back from Washington yesterday."

"Hmm. And what did Coe find out?"

"He thinks we'll have more troops here by the first warm weather, sir. Washington takes a lot of convincin', though. The Major has backed Coe every chance, but you know how it is."

Jim Wade said gently, "Any man is goin' to fight for food for his family, even an Indian."

"I hope they don't until we get the troops,"

Tom said. "It does look bad, though. Last week the chiefs told Murrel, the acting agent, that they couldn't hold the young bucks down much longer. They're talking war and they mean it. This week's beef issue was nearly a riot. Next week the Major will call a company out and bluff 'em down, but that can't last forever."

"A damn good trouncin' is what those Cheyennes need," Mr. Tressel growled.

"Not with a short two companies, sir," Tom said, shaking his head. "By the way, the Major said you were staying with him tonight."

"No, no, thank you. I'm taking early stage tomorrow for Sill. When a man gets to be a Major, he won't breakfast before eight and by that time I'll be on my way."

Jim told me later that evening that the friendship between Mr. Tressel and Major Corning was genuine and lasting. Mr. Tressel was civil to all Yankees, but he chose southern men as his friends. Major Corning was a Yankee, had put in four years in the War Between the States as a lieutenant and had earned his promotion in the Tennessee campaign. Yet he and Mr. Tressel, who fought with Early, had founded a deep if cross-grained friendship upon interminable arguments of the war.

Later the four of us walked over to the Hall, which was behind the Adjutant's building. The garrison ambulances were gathering the late comers from the officers' homes on the east side of the parade grounds. Jim fell in beside me as we walked, and he pointed out the buildings, some of which were new and not yet completed. The officers' quarters had burned the fall before and new stone construction waited upon warm weather. Trees had been planted and in summer this must have been a green and pleasant oasis of civilization. We passed enlisted men, both Negroes and whites, on their way to and from the sutler's bar at Edmonds. More of them knew Jim Wade than knew Mr. Tressel, and their greetings were informal and friendly.

The Hall was a stone affair and for what purpose it was used other than dancing I never did learn. The hum of music and talking could be heard through the closed door. Inside, an orderly took our coats and we entered the long room which held the dance floor. It was decorated with papers streamers and Japanese lanterns, and its walls, jammed with men, hid the military orchestra at the far end. There seemed to be more civilians than army men, although I later learned that a party of officers from Fort Sill had come up for the occasion. Many people were grouped around Major Corning, and it was toward this group we headed. I do not believe I had wholly realized the respect in which my employers were held until I walked through that room beside Jim Wade. Every man there, army officers and civilians, seemed to know him and want to speak to him.

Jim introduced me to Agent and Mrs. Coe, who were talking to the Major, and then to Major Corning himself. He was a bald, taciturn man with refined features and a shy manner, but when Mr. Tressel mentioned that I was associated with the firm he unbent and told me a scurrilous story concerning Mr. Tressel, which Mrs. Coe, much more jolly and pleasant than her serious appearing husband, received with laughter. Then Major Corning, who had arrived only a short time before us, asked Mrs. Coe to dance and they sought the floor. This was a signal, the army men remarked to Jim, that the Major was about to unbend briefly before he retired from the party. The dance with the Agent's wife was routine, traditional, a duty which he bore with a soldier's fortitude, and Mr. Tressel smiled faintly at his friend's discomfort.

There were pretty women and gay gowns, I could see now. With one woman to every ten men, the dances were short and lively and the two homely daughters of an agency employee were being courted to a degree which would have flattered a St. Louis belle.

When the dance ended many couples came over to greet Jim, and while I was still murmuring acknowledgments to introductions, an army man approached and laid a hand on Jim's arm.

He turned and smiled quickly and said, "Evenin', Douglas," and shook hands with a man wearing captain's bars. Captain Douglas Preftake was a burly man, not over-tall, with a squarish, reserved face and chestnut hair and full mustache already graying. He shook my hand warmly, slowly, and said to Jim, "Ellen asked me to bring you over."

"I was savin' the best till the last, Doug," Jim drawled, and took Captain Preftake's arm. Evidently they were old friends, and because I thought this I immediately liked Captain Preftake. His sober manner and literal speech were in contrast to Jim's mocking good humor. We picked our way through the crowded floor to a group of army men, who parted at our approach.

I looked, then, at the most beautiful woman I have ever seen, standing among them. She looked at Jim Wade for a brief instant and then smiled and gave him her hand, and then I heard Captain Preftake's sober voice saying, "Ellen, this is Jim's friend, Joel Hardy. My wife, Mrs. Preftake."

She turned her glance to me and I think I was watching the lamp-glow turn her hair into a live and golden torrent, for it was only when she spoke to me that I noticed the warm black-brown of her eyes and then her smile. I do not think a really beautiful woman ever gets used to the homage men unconsciously pay her in their look and manner, and it was as if Ellen Preftake was proud and humble and a little ashamed that she had made me speechless, for I was.

"You are the Joey that Jim has written us about," she said, and her voice was warm and low and friendly.

Jim said, "And it was a first-class defamin' I gave you too, Joey," and winked at me. He turned to the others and I was introduced. When Jim was finished, the music had started. He raised a hand and said, "And this is the dance I wrote you to save for Joey, Ellen. Joey, this is a garrison honor that Major Corning had to wait three years for, so step lively, boy."

Before I knew it, Mrs. Preftake had put her arm through mine and we went onto the floor and danced. It was brief and breathless and when I took her back to her husband, Jim claimed the next dance over the good-natured protests of the officers.

I stood beside Captain Preftake and watched them, and it gave me a warm feeling that I could not define. Jim Wade was tall and handsome and gay and once he threw back his head and laughed at something Mrs. Preftake had said. She was straight and clean looking in a dress of some maroon stuff that clung to her long slim legs as Jim whirled her. Looking at them the thought suddenly occurred to me that this picture was right, and that these two belonged together, and I know that everyone in that room watching them thought the same thing. It was the natural thing to think — until I remembered that this was a married woman.

I looked at Captain Preftake, who had ceased talking to light a cigar. He discarded his match and said, "I'm ready for punch. Are you, Joel?" I said I was and we worked our way to the punch bowl which was backed by a smiling Negro.

Jim soon found us and took me along to meet some of the officers' wives. After that Tom Wynant, who was more a connoisseur of garrison dances than Jim, took me in hand and I met a half-dozen girls, all pleasant to talk to and look at; and for the next two hours I joined the sport, for the act of trying to get in my bid for a dance and having it accepted in the face of a dozen simultaneous bids was sport. Besides, the fact of my being a newcomer was an advantage I used shamelessly.

Later, at one of the pauses in the music, I was on my way to join Jim, who was at the punch bowl. Almost there, Tom Wynant put a hand on my arm and stopped me and introduced me to four civilians, all of whom were government contractors, he said. There was a Mr. Groom, a Mr. Hampton, a Mr. Young-blood and a Mr. Paddock. It was Mr. Paddock whom I met last, just as Jim stepped up beside me. Mr. Santee Paddock had a long face, a flat face, bisected by a palc full mustache, and his eyes at the outer corners were hooded by folds of flesh, giving them a secretive, wary expression. When he removed the cigar from his mouth and smiled as he shook hands with me, his great strong teeth were almost as yellow as his hair.

"Hod'y'do, Mr. Teller," he said to me.

Tom Wynant said easily, "Mr. Hardy is the name, Santee."

"I beg your pardon," Mr. Santee Paddock said quickly, and his gaze shuttled to Jim beside me. "I thought this was young Mr. Teller, the Secretary's son. They told me the Secretary thought so much of the Canadian Cattle Company's prospects he wanted to get his family in it too, Lieutenant."

There was an unpleasant silence for only a brief part of a second and then Jim Wade drawled from beside me, "That's a pardonable mistake, Santee. As a matter of fact, Mr. Hardy is connected with the government. The War Department didn't think he was too young to send out on a little matter of private investigation."

Santee Paddock's eyes grew a little more wary,

I thought. He looked carefully at me and then back at Jim and said, "That so? An investigator."

"Yes, sir," Jim went on. "There's been some ugly rumors reachin' Washington, he tells me, about beef contractin' for the army out this way."

Santee said meagerly, "What were these rumors?"

"Why, sir," Jim said gently, "there's a rumor around, that after a cowboy read off the lowest figure for the government beef bids to a herd of cattle over at the Darlington agency, those steers got so purse-proud, sir, that they won't speak to their Texas relatives."

There was no silence this time. Everyone within earshot — and there were many — burst into laughter. One of the contractors, Mr. Groom, laughed until he choked and had to be slapped on the back. Mr. Santee Paddock, with an utterly expressionless face, dropped his cigar and walked away.

Jim's face was barely contained, little dancing lights in his gray eyes the only clue to his amusement. He nodded to the others and led me over to the punch bowl.

"Who is this Santee Paddock?" I asked, for I did not fully understand this yet.

"He's a beef contractor to the army and the Indians, and a rich one," Jim said.

"What did he mean by calling me Mr. Teller?"

"That was his own sorry way of tellin' me that I was playin' more politics than luck in getting our lease."

"Are we?"

"No, sir. Mr. Santee Paddock had a nice little business on the reservation before we came, and he wanted our lease. He missed the train and I didn't." He handed me a glass of punch. "I'm right sorry, Joey, about that. Santee generally has the manners to confine his insults to me."

"It doesn't matter," I blurted out. I felt a hot and loyal affection for Jim Wade, then; he was a host apologizing for the bad manners of an uninvited guest. He had taken in the situation in one brief second, accepted the insult himself, and returned it compounded to Santee Paddock, and I was grateful. I said, "Thanks, Jim. I . . . guess I wasn't expecting talk like that."

Jim Wade said something to me then that I've never forgotten, and he said it almost inaudibly, as if he were addressing himself.

"That's true, Joey. But the day has got to come when you can expect talk like that. And when it comes, it's a right comfortable feelin' to know that the other man is just scratchin' sand, because it's not the truth."

Others came up to us then and Jim drifted off with them while I strolled up the floor. The music stopped, presently, and one of the fiddlers rose and announced that the next dance was ladies' choice. The announcement was greeted by hand-clapping and laughter.

What I did next can only be put down to my youth and my arrogance. A couple had paused almost in front of me, and the girl was one of the ugly daughters of an agency employee. I had danced with her once, simply out of sport, and was rewarded by having to reciprocate in an outrageous flirtation. It was my vanity that bred an immediate fear, for I was certain that she would turn now and, seeing me, remember our words and choose me as her partner. I did not propose to be thus corralled. Already the ladies were walking up and down in front of the line of laughing men, even going among them in search of their favorite partners. I knew if I were to act, I must do so immediately.

I turned and shouldered through the men to the very wall. It did not occur to me to walk up or down the room and emerge where I would not be so close to the girl I was trying to avoid; no, I had to hide. I found a door in front of me, and not even caring what it opened onto I eased it ajar and slipped through and shut it behind me. I was in a long corridor running parallel with the dance room. A single lamp was turned low in a wall bracket and I looked up the hall.

And in that hushed half-darkness, I saw two figures, those of Jim Wade and Ellen Preftake. Her arms were about his neck, his about her waist, and they were kissing passionately, lingeringly.

I do not know what I thought; I only know that I wanted to get out of there. I stepped back into the room and was immediately collared by the girl I was hoping to avoid.

That dance never remained in my memory. When it was over, I found Tom Wynant and told him that the stage ride had tired me and that I was leaving. I got my coat and walked across the deserted parade ground to my room, a burning disgust within me.

Once in my room I sat on the bed and considered what I had seen. Fifteen minutes ago I, with the extravagant loyalty of my years, would have been willing to die for Jim Wade.

On this evening I had met the most beautiful and lovely woman of my life. Now, Jim Wade seemed only a cheap and traitorous blackguard and Ellen Preftake a light woman who had betrayed her marriage oath. There was no mercy in my reasoning. Had not Jim Wade shaken hands with Captain Preftake and spoken to him in utter friendliness? And had not

41

Captain Preftake regarded Jim with a quiet affection a man saves for his friends, and which no man can entirely hide? I remembered that briefly eloquent look Ellen Preftake had given Jim the first moment I saw her, and I read into it all the duplicity of her sex. Jim Wade had betrayed a friend in sneaking unmanliness. Ellen Preftake was dishonest, a liar in thought and deed, and a loose woman. I believe I had never felt more lonely and bitter in my life than I did when I reviewed the evening. I thought, too, of how right Elizabeth had been to try and dissuade me from coming here.

When the first shock of it was gone, my thoughts turned to Jim again. I saw him in a new light now; he was a gaudy Texas bravo who had succeeded by brass and bluff and double-dealing, and I hoped I would not have to see him again. Mr. Tressel would be leaving for Fort Sill in the morning, and Jim would be leaving for the northeast corner of our range with a wagon load of grub for a new line camp. Why shouldn't I stay late in bed, until Jim was gone?

I did stay in bed next morning, but at the last moment, hearing voices in the wagon yard below, I went to the window.

Jim was helping the hostler hitch up the team to a borrowed spring wagon in the bright winter sunlight, and he was whistling a thin tune which he embroidered by trills and arpeggios. He was coatless, the cuffs of his undersleeves showing beneath his blue-checked flannel shirt.

Finished hitching up, he tied his horse to the end gate of the wagon, threw his saddle atop the load, and climbed into the wagon.

He drove out with a shout to the horses, and the last I saw of him he was standing up in the wagon warding off the snowballs pelted at him by the blacksmith and his helper.

I told myself then that I was working for Mr. Tressel, and only Mr. Tressel. I was done with Jim Wade.

Two

I spent an hour that morning in the office of Edmonds Brothers with Mr. Robert Edmonds, who advised me where to post my notices for bidding and told me of the service I might expect from the likely bidders. Mr. Santee Paddock, he said, had the greatest facilities for delivering the posts and freighting the wire from Caldwell, but the circumstances of the situation would exclude him. Mr. Edmonds told me this in a dry, amused manner, indicating he knew our attitude toward Paddock. Partly out of curiosity, partly out of the desire to get the background of my job in its entirety, I asked Mr. Edmonds, "What circumstances, sir?"

Mr. Edmonds looked at me carefully and pulled his ear. "Didn't Jim tell you, after last night?"

That talk was around already, then. "He and Mr. Tressel both left before I got up," I explained.

Mr. Edmonds shifted his comfortable bulk in his chair, put his hand on the back of his neck and slowly ran his palm over his bald head and down his face to his cleft chin, which he held delicately between his thumb and index finger for a moment before settling his hand to his lap. It was a gesture he made whenever he was embarrassed or undecided; and afterward it was one I always associated with this likable man.

"Santee is a customer of mine, Joel," he said, and his voice held a careful neutrality.

"Then tell me what Jim thinks, not what you think."

He smiled faintly, considering this, and finally nodded assent. What Jim thought, Mr. Edmonds said, was that Mr. Santee Paddock was a clever and dangerous man whose plans Jim had first interrupted and then thwarted. Before our leases had been signed by the Cheyenne and Arapaho chiefs Santee had been a power in this land. He had grazed his own herds free on Indian grass because he was the largest beef contractor to the Fort and the Agency. Moreover, he had leased Indian land to which he had no title to adventurous cattlemen willing to pay him hard cash for grass and protection against the Indians. He kept the Indians reasonably quiet and unprotesting at this trespass by giving them whiskey, forbidden guns and cull beef. His success in the past lay in that he kept the Indians disunited by fostering quarrels between their many factions. There were always malcontents and young rebels willing to lease him their undefined share of grass in exchange for food and whiskey, and his own roughs kept out cattlemen who would not pay him tribute.

Jim Wade had changed this arrangement by the process of cutting around Santee to pay the elected chiefs liberal grass money, by seeking legal sanction from the government for his leases, and by moving in crews who were unafraid of Santee's riffraff or the malcontent Indians. But Santee had not ceased his tireless scheming, and as long as our company leases were not fully sanctioned by the government, he was a menace. In short, Santee was patient, powerful and unforgiving; if he could channel the Indians' rising dissatisfaction with the government into a protest against us, then we would be destroyed by them or by the government. In either event, Santee would have his revenge, and perhaps the return of the old order. Or so Jim Wade thought, Mr. Edmonds said.

Mr. Edmonds had progressed this far when Lieutenant Tom Wynant entered the office and informed me he had a horse waiting outside and that I was to accompany him to the weekly beef issue to the Indians. I did not consider my liking for Tom had been influenced by Jim Wade, so I readily agreed, thanked Mr. Edmonds for his advice and information, and went along with Tom, willing enough to put my business off for a few hours.

In daylight, the garrison grounds were more impressive than I had thought them. The buildings were of brick and stone, flanking four sides of the parade ground, the only frame buildings except the stables to the north and west being the Edmonds post and residence next it. There were several private dwellings for the married officers. We mounted just as a troop of blue-clad cavalry in greatcoats, sabers clanking and sleek horses trotting smartly, came out of the garrison grounds headed for the issue corral two miles to the west. This was Major Corning's threat to the malcontent Indians, and a capable one it seemed.

We rode slowly out of the grounds. Darlington, the agency town across the river, lay ranked beyond the bare trees of the Canadian bottomland, and the smoke from half a hundred chimneys hung in a flat lucent streamer of blue above the town. The sunlight on the snow was dazzling, and as we angled down the long sloping hill to the river I began to make out the Indians filing across the sandy bed of the Canadian from Darlington. Beyond

47

them, north of the agency, hundreds of gray teepees dotted the large shallow bowl of prairie to the distant ridge.

To my surprise, upon reaching the issue corrals I saw that half a company of infantry had been drawn up on the slope above the corral. Their rifles were stacked in a straight row to the west of the dismounted cavalry.

Below the huge pole corral filled with bawling beef the mass of Indians was gathered. They made a wild and colorful picture, the men on horses and clotted in small groups, the women and children afoot, many of them seated on skins. Whether Arapaho or Cheyenne, they favored the gaudiest of blankets and clothes and seemed to mix without regard to tribe. Already, a hundred small fires had been built and the children and women were scouring the timber on the river bank for fuel. Save for the absence of teepees, it might have been a great tribal council, and Tom told me that most of the Indians had been camped there since sunup.

When I expressed curiosity as to their dress and their appearance, Tom excused himself and rode over to the commander of the cavalry troop. He talked with him a moment, and then the captain raised his hand in greeting to me. I recognized him then as Captain Preftake. Tom returned, saying we had the captain's permission to ride down among the Indians.

Already, soldiers were riding among them, handing out slips of paper which would be redeemed when they were issued their beef, so as to forestall all complaint. We joined a pair of these soldiers and I had a closer view of the Indians. The Cheyennes were easy to identify after Tom pointed pointed out that they were leaner of build, sterner of mien and altogether more warlike than the Arapahos. Men and women both wore a jumble of Indian and white man's clothes. Some wore buckskin under their blankets, and the more bead work embroidered upon it, the more prosperous the owner seemed. As we rode among them, they paid no attention to us, except to regard us with stolid and indifferent hostility. The men said nothing when their claim slips were issued, accepting them without even a grunt of recognition. Once a young Cheyenne buck standing by his paint pony turned to us and said something and spat, but we pretended not to hear. There were not many guns in sight. Occasionally, an Indian in white man's apparel, a hat riding squarely on his head above the twin ropes of hair that lay on his coat lapels, wound be seen among them. Some of the men wore an eagle feather in their scalp locks. The Indian police in their blue coats sporting the big nickeled star above the heart rode back and forth among them.

When we turned and rode back up the slope, I looked at the handful of soldiers and first realized the precariousness of the white man's position in this country. They seemed a pitiful few, even when their numbers were swelled by the numerous civilians from the post, some of whom had ridden up in buggies and on horseback to witness the issue.

When the issue began, bedlam reigned. As a steer broke out of one of the corral gates, two Indians, or less often a lone one, would give chase. The object, I learned later, was not to catch the steer, but to hunt it as they had hunted the buffalo of a decade ago. With a wild whoop, a rider would put about after the steer, crouching along his pony's neck. If he had a gun, he would shoot, being careful to only would the animal and not kill it. The chase might lead down across the river or even into the streets of Darlington before the steer, too weak to run further, went down. Then the buck would dispatch him and ride off, leaving the butchering for his woman and children. There were bows and arrows, spears, knives and guns used, although Tom said the Indians were careful not to exhibit too many guns lest the white man know they were all armed.

"And they are," Tom said. "It's hard to get ammunition, but when the time comes, they'll have it and for a lot of guns, too."

It was a cruel and savage sight, and it took a strong stomach to watch it. But the government had wisely ordained that it should not be stopped, as it provided an outlet for the warring and hunting instincts of a fighting and hunting people whose food, the buffalo, was long since gone. The young bucks had only this poor means of proving their hunting prowess, and then it was only once a week and with a ridiculous substitute for wild game.

Only once did trouble flare up, and it was handled coolly by the soldiers. Two young Cheyennes, claiming three steers which were loosed from the corral chute, settled on one rangy beef and by expert riding turned and drove him up the hill toward the soldiers. With an Indian hugging each flank, and he was being guided directly toward the rank of infantry men. An angry shouting rose among the soldiers, who saw what was coming and understood the intentions of the two bucks.

It was then Captain Preftake spurred his horse and cut over toward the approaching Indians. He drew rein and I saw him raise a pistol and take careful aim. The Indians, sensing what he was about to do, shouted and veered sharply to the left, so that the steer was heading for the cavalry troop. Captain Preftake's arm moved in a steady arc and he shot. The steer's knees folded and he catapulted into the nearest Indian pony, which went down with his rider.

The fallen Indian picked himself up and shouted angrily at Captain Preftake, who coolly wheeled his horse and returned to his men. It was a steady piece of shooting and averted an incident that might have developed into real trouble.

Soon sickened of the scene, I left Tom, who was talking with some of his fellow officers, and rode over to pay my respects to Mr. Robert Edmonds' wife, who was watching from a buggy. Afterward, I saw Santee Paddock alone in a top buggy just beyond hers. I do not know what prompted me to do what I did next. Perhaps it was a simple protest against Jim Wade. If Jim Wade did not like the man, then perhaps I would. I thought of what Mr. Edmonds had told me Jim thought about him, and it was in my mind now that Jim Wade's opinion of a man did not have to be infallible, or even necessarily true.

His greeting showed no enmity and gave me courage, for it was affable. I dismounted and came over to his buggy.

"Watching the weekly butcher show, Mr. Hardy?" he inquired, smiling. He had learned my name, anyway, I thought. He waved his ever-present cigar at the scene. "Queer how those black devils will build a fire right there at the kill and eat, isn't it? Tradition, I suppose. I saw three of them kill a beef on the parade ground one morning and they'd have eaten it right there if Major Corning hadn't had them chased out."

He inquired after Mr. Tressel's departure and asked if the firm had stationed me here for good. It was the chance to bring up my business, and I told him that I was waiting to receive and award bids for fence posts and the freighting of the wire. His face showed an immediate interest.

"That'll be considerable of a contract," he remarked.

"Yes, sir. With the bonds to post it will run into quite an outlay of money, sir."

"I doubt if you'll find that one party can handle it," he answered easily. "Two or three men throwing together might swing it, but down this way we're far from credit sources, Mr. Hardy."

This was the opening for which I had been waiting, and I took my courage in hand.

"Is there any reason why you shouldn't submit a bid, Mr. Paddock?" I asked eagerly. I saw the look of controlled amazement flood his face, and I pushed my case. "You've got the men and the credit, I understand."

He turned his face then and spat out an inch of cigar which he had bitten off, but when he turned to me again he regarded me with flint-hard eyes.

"Mr. Hardy, either you are a young fool or you've been misinformed, which I doubt. I would not contract to cut the posts to burn Jim Wade alive. Good day, sir."

He whipped up his team before I could take my foot from his buggy step, leaving me to stand there blazing with anger and shame. That men could be polite and still hate each other passionately was something I learned that day. But what angered me most was that Jim Wade had been right.

I resolved then that I would get my business done as soon as possible and get on to Texas and Mr. Tressel. Within three days I had received all the bids but one.

The day following the beef issue I spent the morning hunting turkey with Tom Wynant in the Canadian bottoms. I returned in the afternoon to hear that Captain Preftake had been ordered north with a troop of cavalry on the strength of the stage driver's account that the Boomers had pushed across the Kansas line again into the Territory. There were two notes waiting for me at the hotel, both from Mrs. Preftake. One invited me to dinner at their home that evening. The other, written after Captain Preftake had received his orders, said that the invitation still held, and that we would dine alone.

I did not intend to spend an evening alone with her, and I wrote a note pleading a bad cold. It was as formal a note as the outraged morality of my years could dictate. Tomorrow evening was to be spent at the Agent's home, and with luck I would not have to see Mrs. Preftake before I left the morning after.

Fortune did not favor me.

When, on the last night of my stay at Fort Reno, I arrived after dark at the agency residence in Darlington and was welcomed by jolly Mrs. Coe, she led me straight to the parlor. Ellen Preftake was seated on the sofa. I contrived to work up a respectable cough while being introduced to Mr. and Mrs. Murrel, agency people, and my greeting to Mrs. Preftake was only polite. I sat down upon the sofa beside her, so I would not have to look at her, for I knew that if I were to watch her loveliness all my resolutions would melt. She was dressed in a blue, yellow-spangled dress with long sleeves and high neck. There was nothing about her that I had always associated with married women — matronliness, preoccupation with her home and a love of talking about her husband. She sat there, straight and slim and chaste looking, and talked of Indian affairs with Mr. Coe and the other guests, and not once did she mention Captain Preftake, except to politely regret he was gone. What gossip she reported was amusing and not malicious. Her talk was altogether feminine, but she seemed to understand the ultimate courtesy of talking to people about themselves and their interests, and in spite of myself I found that before the evening was over I had told the company my own business and our plans and hopes.

I had come into the Coes' parlor determined to hate her presence, the evening and the luck that had brought us together. When it came time to go I was astonished that I had been having a good time. At Mrs. Coe's prompting, Mr. Coe was about to send a man with an agency ambulance to drive Mrs. Preftake home when Ellen said, "But Joel will drive me home, won't you, Joel?" I could not refuse with civility, and I seconded her suggestion.

After saying goodbye to our hosts, we turned out through the dark town on the Reno road in my rented buggy. We were made snug with robes and the horses were stepping lively. A waning moon touched the road and the trees with the frost of its light and we could hear the Indian dogs over in the camp to the north lifting their mournful din to the stars.

Ellen Preftake said suddenly, "Up early tomorrow, Joel?"

"In time for the Fort Sill stage."

"Too early to go for a drive tonight? It's lovely."

My impulse was to answer that the day had tired me, but a stubborn wish to prove to myself that I was impervious to her charm made me answer that I would like to see the country in the moonlight. We crossed the river and took the river road toward the military forest reserve several miles up the river. Neither of us spoke for a long time, and Mrs. Preftake was the first to break the silence.

"Have you a girl at home, Joel?" she asked.

I did not want to discuss Elizabeth Lowell with this woman. Somehow it did not seem proper, and I answered stiffly, "Yes."

"In school still?"

"Yes."

"Do you want to marry her?"

"I – I – yes."

"Does she like this country, Joel, and does she like your work?" she persisted in a low voice.

I said briefly, "She hates it. She goes to school in Boston and when we are married we will live in St. Louis."

"I know. She thinks this country is rough and crude and without any of the refinements a woman wants, doesn't she?"

I bridled. "Isn't it?"

"I don't know," Ellen Preftake said slowly. "I might as well be in Boston as here. It's not crude to me. I came out of a quiet home into

57

this quiet one. If the Indians were taken away and all the talk about them were to stop, and if I did not have to make the stage ride to meet the Kansas City train, I might be living in the East."

I considered this, thinking of St. Louis and home. "But it isn't the same. There is music there and people and clubs and balls and fine horses and Sunday drives."

"All dull," she murmured.

"Not as dull as a five-day stage ride," I answered quickly. "Not as dangerous as listening to booze-crazy cowboys brawling in the street. Not dusty, not muddy, not so forlorn as this empty prairie."

She laughed softly and I turned to look at her. She was wearing a heavy cape with a fur collar that softly framed her face. Her profile was as cleanly modelled as a cameo, serene in repose. But there was an underlying restlessness in her voice and in her laugh that was almost wild.

"But the other is too safe," she said finally.

"That's what we want," I answered in amazement. "Some day they will build a railroad through here. There will be towns and farms and security from the Indians."

"Not 'we,' Joel," she said.

"Not 'we' what?"

"Don't say 'we' want it, because I don't." She

turned to me and said swiftly, "My great-aunt went to California in '49 Joel. She was a grown girl then and she ran away and found a family leaving from Independence who would take her West for a sum. She stole a diamond stickpin from a gambler to pay her way. In San Francisco she married the mate of a China Clipper and they lost their first baby in a fight with pirates off Sumatra after her husband had been given a command. Five years later they settled on the west coast of Central America. I've read her letters, Joel. They hacked a plantation out of the jungle with seventy slaves that worshipped them. She had eleven children and a house as big as a town and when she died even the Indians came down from the hills and left presents at her grave. She chewed tobacco and was killed by a jaguar and" — she turned away from me and settled back in the seat — "she lived."

"Is that what you want?" I asked brusquely.

"Sometimes," she said. "Especially when I'm cutting out the pattern for a new dress that every woman in the garrison knows I'm going to wear. And when."

Before I had an answer framed she said, "Shall we turn around? It's late."

I swung the horses off the road and the thin crust of snow crackled sharply under the wheels on the turn. Her talk had affected me strangely, communicating a part of her discontent to me. A pair of coyotes far down the river bluff sent their quavering cry across the winter night touching it with a wild melancholy.

"What is it they try to tell us?" Ellen Preftake asked, listening. "It seems as if they know an unbearable truth that makes us afraid when we listen to it."

I said in a matter-of-fact voice, "They are cowards."

"Maybe that is the truth they know."

I glanced obliquely at her, troubled by the strangeness in her, and found her smiling at me.

"Dear Joel," she said softly. "Everything is simple, isn't it?"

"I guess so. Eating and sleeping and doing your work. They're simple, I suppose," I said, half in anger.

"And that's all."

I said without thinking, "Not all of us can be like Jim Wade." I could have bitten my tongue when it was out. She did not betray by so much as a look or gesture that this reference to Jim might hold a special meaning. Instead of being ashamed, I was angry at her coolness.

"Yes, Jim Wade," she murmured. "Do you know how we met him?"

I said I didn't.

"He delivered some contract beef to the post

here one spring two years ago. A bully of a quartermaster's sergeant and two troopers did not approve his count and called him a liar. When Douglas rode past the corral Jim was sitting on the top bar, smoking, nursing a black eye. The three soldiers were stretched out in the dirt of the corral. Jim looked at Douglas and said, 'If my arithmetic don't suit you, Captain, then careful how you correct it.'"

"I don't see how that makes him a better man," I said gruffly.

"No. I didn't suppose you would," was her gentle answer.

We were silent afterward. I was thinking that I was glad of this ride. Ellen Preftake had changed for me, simply because I thought I understood her now. She was weak and discontented, not vicious. Where before I hated her, I do not think I did then; I pitied and understood her, but my opinion of her was unchanged. It gave me a kind of oblique understanding of the events leading up to what I saw at the garrison dance. Jim Wade had taken advantage of a woman too romantic and too weak to resist him.

Three

Mr. Tressel met me at the crossing of the Red River and we set out upon our trip across the North Texas counties. In the days that we were separated, Mr. Tressel had done considerable riding and talking, and the results confirmed what Jim had told him in Reno, he said. The market for the coming summer looked extremely shaky. The Kansas quarantine law, which prohibited the entry of Texas cattle into Kansas except from December 1 to March 1, for fear of spreading Texas fever, had depressed the market. The end of the big trail drives from Texas was in sight; and all the talk among the Texas ranchers of starting a new trail, the National, which would leave the Texas panhandle and travel through Colorado, skirting Kansas, was merely whistling in the dark. The unpleasant fact they had to face was that the upper markets in the northern country had fallen off during the winter; not a northern buyer had appeared at the stockmen's meetings in Texas this winter. It was the big holding lease, where Texas cattle could be wintered and the possibility of them spreading the dread Texas fever eliminated, that stood to profit by the death of the trail drive and the coming of the quarantine law, and we held the biggest lease.

It was my conservative youth speaking when I asked, "Then Jim won't buy much this year?"

"Sixty thousand head."

I remembered the figure of last year, and this exceeded it; and I protested. "With no northern market? He must be" — I was going to say "crazy," but I amended it — "well, a gambler."

Mr. Tressel chuckled. "He is, and I told him so. He only said, 'Those ranchers in the north aren't going to take up a hoe, Harry, and meat is still pretty good eating.' I guess that's all there is to say."

"Not all," I said. "There's something to be said for waiting for a better market — or even for selling out at the peak. Especially when our leases are shaky."

"We're buying, Joey, buying," Mr. Tressel said, "Every business man in Caldwell with a dollar in his pocket wants Jim to take it. They believe in him. And with few trail herds making up, we've got our pick of beef. This year we name our own price for the best."

He said nothing about our leases, however,

and I got the impression that he did not want to talk about them. And his quoting of Jim galled me. Perhaps the merchants of Caldwell would not have been so anxious to invest their money with a man of his character if they knew about him what I knew. I was unforgiving still.

We moved east and south with our buckboard and team, into the bare plains country of scrub mesquite and grass as limitless as the ocean — and almost as treeless. I had thought of the Kansas prairies as vast and endless, but the plains of Texas defied comprehension. The sky was higher, the air clearer, the distances stunning. Day after day the horizon receded before us, unchanged, featureless, sometimes as flat as if it were surveyed and graded. Behind us it was the same; it was as if we were on a great treadmill, our horses pushing the earth back in an endless belt to the back horizon only to have it appear on the forward horizon while we remained stationary. Herd after herd of identical fat cattle heightened this impression.

This was really not so, for Mr. Tressel recognized landmarks, and occasionally the earth would break for a creek and some trees and here we might find a ranch house. Mr. Tressel would know whose it was and we would stop and, if business was in order, change to saddle horses for the closer inspection of cattle. We were welcomed everywhere, feasted and entertained until what I thought was a business trip turned into a grand tour of frontier banquets, fine horses and entertainment.

We saw towns too, tiny wind-scoured crossroad settlements of a few stores and a saloon and maybe a hotel. Nobody ever explained to me why settlers picked this spot in the great ocean plain on which to build towns, for they were dreary, lonesome and ugly. It was in one of these small towns, the third week in March, that we learned of Mr. Cleveland's inauguration as President. What was more important to us, he had selected a western man, Mr. Lamar, as his Secretary of Interior, and Mr. Tressel assured me that this appointment was to our advantage.

The spring rains caught us deep into the upper tiers of Texas counties. We were in good cattle country now, where fence marked out the great cattle holdings. Our heaviest buying was done here and Mr. Tressel one day suddenly announced that I was to look over and contract for a herd of a thousand two-year-olds while he saw to some other business. It was the first time I had been trusted with this end of our business and, in consequence, I was very exacting on that day. But Mr. Tressel was an expert teacher, and although I had never handled a rope, never broken a wild horse, never drawn my thirty a month as a trail hand, I could look over cattle and accurately guess their weight and condition, spot their defects, judge to a reasonable nicety the most I could pay for them and clear up the details of delivery. My memory was an encyclopedia of brands, and although I had seldom seen the Brazos River, I could name almost every brand that bordered it. I would make Jim Wade a good employee, even if I disliked him, I reflected.

We had reached the eastern limit of our journey and now turned west to complete the circle, just as the windy Texas spring came upon us. As soon as the grass was up, our herds would start up the trails to the Indian Territory.

Mr. Tressel was looking forward to our reunion with Jim Wade and began to talk about it. I had succeeded in putting him at the back of my mind for more than a month now, and I did not look upon the meeting with much relish. True, time had cooled my outrage a little, but had not lessened it.

So close to our planned scheduled had both Mr. Tressel and Jim kept that we arrived at the county seat of Stonewall County within a few hours of one another. We were first and when we pulled up at the hotel tie rail in our mud-spattered buckboard, an enormous man rose from his chair on the sidewalk and shouted greetings to us.

This was Mr. Ketro, Mr. Tressel said, an old

friend of his who had a ranch now on the Double Mountain fork of the Brazos. We adjourned to the saloon out of the wind to talk cattle. Since Mr. Ketro, on account of his girth, could not comfortably belly up to the bar, we took seats. His first words were to inquire profanely after Jim and to invite us all to his ranch, both in the same breath, and Mr. Tressel accepted the invitation. I learned minutes later that Mr. Tressel had dropped a letter to his friend a month ago asking that ten thousand head of mixed two- and three-year-olds, be reserved for him. The business had been done by letter, the cattle bought sight unseen, and it was only after that that I realized Mr. Ketro was Mr. Tressel's oldest friend.

He was a mountainous man in muddy boots who never spoke beneath a roar. His round and ruddy face, his merry blue eyes were never still under his tatterdemalion hat. He entered this frontier saloon like a whirlwind and left in his wake numbed eardrums and faces weary from laughing. A man so transparently simple and exuberant could affect people in two ways; he could be a tonic or he could be a booming nerve-shattering tornado. To Mr. Tressel, mild-mannered and quiet, he was the former, but to me he was the latter. He drank his whiskey not from a whiskey glass but from a water tumbler, and did not even stop his torrent of speech to catch his breath afterward. At present he was incensed at the threatened Kansas quarantine laws and he beat the table until I heard it crack. Every man in the saloon, a few cowboys, was his audience whether or not he liked it.

Mr. Tressel was chuckling silently at Mr. Ketro, who had kicked back his chair and was standing up to emphasize his point, hammering the table.

"Why, damit, damit, Harry, it's a plot to ruin us!" he bellowed. "Those Kansas men want our cattle shut out and the market closed. Then they'll turn around and sell the cattle we sold them to the northern ranchers for ten times what they paid us!" Crash! went his fist. "When they're sold out, you'll see that quarantine law by the boards, sir! Why, it stands to reason" – his tirade went on, but my glance had shuttled to the batwing doors.

They had exploded apart to let in a man on the run, mouthing a wild Confederate yell. It was Jim Wade, and with one long leap he vaulted to Mr. Ketro's shoulders. Mr. Ketro did not even stagger against Jim's hundred and eighty pounds; he put both fat arms up and hoisted Jim off his shoulders as easily as if he had been a baby, and then they were locked in a wrestling match that upset the table on me and threw me against the wall. It ended in less than a minute, with Jim, laughing breathlessly, under Mr. Ketro's knee. He picked Jim up and set him on the bar and bawled for drinks, and Jim Wade was with us again.

I realized then that I had never seen Jim Wade in his element, and that he was in it now. Save for leather *chaparejos*, which I never saw him wear, no matter how cold it was nor how thick the brush he must ride through, he looked like any of the other cowboys in the saloon. A wiry black beard stubble darkened his face, making his teeth whiter as he smiled at me. He wore two shirts, the cotton one under the flannel, and a black silk neckerchief. His eyebrows and every crease in his clothes were sifted over with a fine dust that rode the spring wind. His boots were caked with mud, but his spurs were clean and small. His cedar-handled gun was worn in a closed holster, the flap buttoned.

He told me, when Mr. Ketro's talk had been dammed by a glass to his mouth, that he and two of his men had brought down three hundred head of horses from the lease to outfit our trail herds. He was friendly and polite and asked how I liked Texas and I said stiffly that I liked it and how were all my friends at Fort Reno?

"They're fine, Joey. Mr. Santee Paddock sent his regards."

"Oh," I said, wondering if Jim knew of my last meeting with Paddock. "You talked with him."

"Yes, sir. I walked right into an Indian scare. Some Cheyennes had threatened to kill the agent that day, and everybody expected trouble. To keep from broodin' I sat in on a poker game with Santee and won four hundred dollars from him. I won more than that, but I refused to take his check. Just to get even with me he ruined the credit in Arkansas City of two of your post contractors, Joey. I had to go up to straighten it out for them in order to get the posts. That's one lesson in gamblin' I never expected to learn," he added ruefully.

I was going to ask about the Preftakes, when Mr. Ketro interrupted. "Jim, Harry, here, wrote sayin' if the election went the way it should you'd want another five thousand head. I don't read politics much but when I saw Mr. Lamar's name as Mr. Cleveland's Secretary I sent the wagons out. Was I right?"

"Our stockholdin' Senator writes so," Jim answered.

"Good. Any more word on the lease business?"

Jim shook his head, smiling faintly. "They're tryin' to forget us, I reckon."

"But you're stockin' up. Good. It ain't as if we had a man in Lamar's place that was as a New England farmer. When one of them Yankees read a lease has been signed on enough land to swamp four of their states, they don't believe it.

It don't make their kind of sense."

"I've met Lamar," Mr. Tressel put in. "He's a western man and understands a stockman."

"He's got to," Jim murmured. "This fall I can show the Senator some figures that will read in heavy black ink. If I haven't got a line of Congressmen waitin' to buy stock in the Canadian Cattle Company, then gold isn't the same color on the Potomac as it is on the Cimarron, gentlemen."

"More land?"

"Another million acres," Jim said, laughing suddenly.

I stood gaping, and while they talked on I looked at Jim Wade, and for the first time, I think, I saw the real measure of the man. I knew the risks we were running, and I knew the money we were handling. I knew, too, that if Jim Wade were dressed in a black suit and high collar in the board room of a St. Louis bank talking this kind of figures to other men in black suits and high collars, they would listen with respect. But because I had seen him fondle a woman in a dark hall in an obscure army post, I had lost my sense of proportion. I resolved then that if I were part of something this big, no man would ever be given cause to question my loyalty to Jim Wade, not even myself.

Afterward, Mr. Ketro took us home. Mr.

Tressel and I rode in our buckboard, Ketro riding beside Mr. Tressel, Jim reining in his horse alongside me. It was a windy day, and our road a long one. This was the edge of open range, Mr. Ketro's fence being the last to the west. We drove nine miles after entering his gate and Jim told me that across the Brazos his range ran on for sixty miles into the next county.

The Ketro ranchhouse lay in the Brazos breaks among cottonwoods that were just beginning to green, a big new frame house whose boards had been hauled up from the new Texas and Pacific line to the south. It was big and square and two-storey and painted a white which the blown dust had already ground to a gray color. There was a log bunkhouse and cookshack for the hands between the big house and the corrals, and beyond them was the wooded slope to the grassy bottomlands of the Brazos.

We arrived after dark and were greeted by Mr. Ketro's six girls. Or rather Jim Wade received the real greeting. The oldest girl was Martha, about my age. Jim swung off his horse, picked her up and kissed her, then greeted Mrs. Ketro. The youngsters hung on to Jim and would not even let him get his few belongings which were rolled in the blankets behind his saddle. Later, after we had washed and been shown our rooms and were gathered in the warm kitchen where Jim was trying to shave and talk at the same time, I watched Martha Ketro, who was directing the supper. She was a slight girl with a slim sensitive face and her father's wide blue eyes. Her laughter was quick and infectious, and she could not keep her adoring glance away from Jim Wade. She listened to his easy banter with delight, and was there with a clean towel before he needed it, brought him hot water and a new bar of yellow homemade soap. I thought of Ellen Preftake and reflected that wherever Jim Wade went there was a woman waiting for him, a woman to conquer.

Mrs. Ketro was small and quiet, Martha grown up, and so used to her husband's fury of speech that she could talk below it and be understood and still pay wifely attention. Our supper was a merry one. There was a red tablecloth loaded down with beef and venison, cooked two ways, steaming vegetables from the cold cellar, two kinds of soups, three kinds of breads and rolls, turkey, five jellies and as many sorts of pies. It was a table set in Mr. Ketro's style, and he stated once with a sly twinkle in his eye that with this household of womenfolks he aimed to keep their hours full cooking for him.

After supper, Mr. Ketro passed out cigars

and the men went into the living room where a fire was burning in the huge fireplace. Martha stopped Jim and me and asked us if we would go with her to the Beechams, the nearest neighbor down the Brazos. Because the woman of the house was sick Martha was taking over a quantity of cooked food. She looked at Jim as she asked this, and I know I was included in her invitation only out of politeness. When Jim said he'd like to go, I answered, "Miss Martha, I've driven so far in a buckboard I never want to see one again."

She laughed and said, "You'll go, though, Jim?"

When she had gone Jim looked at me and said, "Too much supper, Joey?"

"You want to be alone with her, don't you?" I asked shortly and walked on into the living room. Jim and Martha left immediately. I visited with the Ketros and Mr. Tressel until the children were all in bed and then I went to the room on the ground floor I was sharing with Jim.

In bed I could not sleep for thinking of him. The question of loyalty to him I had settled with myself this afternoon, and I meant to stick by my decision. But the other part of him, the person side, I could decently criticize, and I was doing so bitterly. I had it all reasoned out that I was little jealous of him, but I knew it was more than that. Martha Ketro was a nice girl, too nice for Jim Wade, and when I remembered that night at the garrison dance I was angry again. If Jim Wade had repaid Douglas Preftake's friendship by philandering with his wife, what would keep him from paying back Mr. Ketro's hospitality in the same coin? And Martha Ketro adored him.

I did not know what time it was when Jim tiptoed into the room, trying not to waken me. He came over to my bed and stood above me, and I timed my breathing to a slow and regular pulse and did not move.

"You liar," Jim said presently and lighted the lamp. I turned over and grinned sheepishly. He stood straight in the orange glow of the lamp, packing his pipe and scowling. When he had lighted up he said, "We pulled taffy, Joey. You missed a right nice time."

"It sounds exciting."

He grinned and said, "We prayed for the health of Mrs. Beecham, who's got a bellyache, and then Uncle Henry broke out a bottle of elderberry wine. I got a middlin' good swallow of it before Uncle Henry said, 'We better go careful, son. We don't want to face the womenfolks too far gone,' and he put the bottle away."

I laughed then in spite of myself. "Why did you go over?"

"Martha promised. Why didn't you?"

"I thought you'd probably like to be alone."

His glance was puzzled. "So you said. Why should I?"

Coupled with what I imagined had gone on between him and Martha and the memory of Ellen Preftake this hypocrisy was too much. Suddenly, I was so angry and headstrong that no memory of his kindness to me, no thought of my job could prevent me from saying what I had to say.

I sat up in bed and said hotly, "To do the same thing with Martha that you did with Mrs. Preftake, of course!"

For one brief second he stood motionless, and then I saw the cold fury crawl into his face. He took the pipe from his mouth with a slow, groping motion and said, "So."

I waited, not afraid to look in his angry eyes, nor was he ashamed to face me.

"You saw something, then?" he asked in a quiet voice.

"At the dance at Reno. In the hall. Yes. I wasn't snooping. I never told anybody."

He was silent a long time, staring at me, the anger draining out of his dark face. "So that's why you don't like me or trust me, Joey?"

"Yes," I replied angrily.

He nodded once and said slowly, "Well, I don't blame you."

He said nothing else, but undressed and blew

out the light and got in his bed. I lay rigid, a thousand thoughts tumbling through my mind, waiting for him to say more. I had seen him only these few hours since that night at Fort Reno, and yet he knew I disliked him. There was the future to think of now, and I knew I would be too proud ever to tell him I was loyal to part of him, the Company part. That made sense to me, but only to me, and the thought of my situation was intolerable.

When I was certain of that I said, "Jim."

"Yes."

"I'm leaving once my work is done at Reno."

"On account of this, Joey?"

"Yes."

"Don't you," he said quietly. "I'd lose my conscience that way. No. You stay." A little while later he added, "Don't you think hard of her, Joe," and after that, perhaps a minute later, "I'm not a triflin' man, Joey, and I aim to show you." That was the closest to an apology he ever came, and that was not close at all. To this I answered nothing, because I was discovering that I liked him.

Four

Two days later Jim and I left for the lease, where the single- and double-wintered beeves must be rounded up, ready to drive up the trail for shipment in the summer. Mr. Tressel was remaining in Texas, first to gather the Ketro herds, and then wait for the delivery of our other herds at Fort Griffin.

It was a ride into unfolding spring, unforgettable and perfect. With only our packhorses for carrying provisions, we traveled north at an easy pace. Save for the crew of one trail herd making up this side of Fort Griffin, the first herd of the season, we saw no one. The new grass was beginning to show in the brown plains, drawn up by a sun whose heat was tempered by cool winds touched with the lush damp smell of far rains. Red River was running high and we had to swim our horses, and after that we were in the Kiowa-Comanche country, the hill slopes greening and come alive with spring.

Jim Wade made me love that country, and in so quiet a way that I never suspected I was being shown. Once we made camp before dusk beside a wide creek hooded by tall blackjacks, and while I gathered wood Jim staked out my horse and disappeared on his own. When he came back in the twilight he was dragging a deer on the deep grass at the end of his rope. He could name all the creeks and landmarks. Here was a camp of some Negro soldiers ambushed by Indians twelve years ago. There was a spring that would kill a steer before he got ten feet away from his drinking place. Riding with him, this empty empire of sun-drenched grass and sky took on some order and reason. In all that long ride, Jim did not once refer to my leaving, which I had threatened. By mutual and unspoken consent, it was forgotten. Nor did he once mention Ellen Preftake.

And then one day we came suddenly upon a fencing crew and it marked the end of our close companionship, for at last we were on our lease. We arrived the next night at one of the company's line camps long after dark and although there was not a dog in camp and we rode up on the thick grass, a lone man hailed us from the darkness, and with a rifle in his hand. He was careful to identify us before he stepped back into the shack and lighted his candle.

This was a strange reception, I thought.

He took our horses and led us to the shack, a small rough affair of a single room built of sod strips and roofed with earth. Four men could sleep in the two double-decker bunks filled with mattresses of buffalo grass. The provisions were stacked and hung from the ridgepole by wire as protection against squirrels and mice. A plateful of cut steaks covered with flour sacking lay on the table, and by the time the cowboy returned, Jim had the tiny stove going and the steaks sizzling in the fry pan.

Jim called the puncher Murdo and he was a tall, saddle-leaned Texan line rider of about Jim's age. Squatting against the wall while we ate, he told us of the progress of the fence building, and deftly Jim maneuvered him around to answering the question which had been troubling me. Why the precaution with which we had just been greeted?

"Just careful," Murdo said, grinning. "I had a bottle broke in my face the other night at the Quartermaster creek shack."

Jim's eyes were suddenly full of sharp, scheming attention, but he said nothing.

Murdo went on. "Whoever done it got sassy and drove off a steer and butchered him just across the line stakes."

"Our steer?"

"I can't say for sure without I see the chunk

he cut out of the hide, the piece with the brand."

"No earmark?"

"The ear was gone, too." Murdo frowned thoughtfully. "I was reasonably sure it was our'n, but you said if we missed a beef now and then to let it ride."

"But I never said that included shooting at us."

"No, you never did."

Jim laid down his fork. "Who was it, some of these hardcases on the wolf?"

"Not this time. It was a Cheyenne. I followed him and got a look at him."

Jim was still now, his face alert, his quizzical glance on Murdo.

"Things are building up, Jim," Murdo said, softly. "You remember how there was always a pack of them Cheyennes hanging around headquarters place beggin' a side of beef or some tobacco? They ain't there any more. They just take the beef on the hoof without botherin' to ask, now."

Jim said nothing more that night, but I knew this was disquieting news to him. We were to learn no more of affairs until we reached headquarters camp, two days later. We nooned on the second day at a meat camp of three families of friendly Arapahos, who had the privilege of hunting on the lease. All around us on that day's ride were fat longhorn steers and a few cows with winterborn calves. They stippled the fawn slopes like pepper scattered over wrapping paper, thicker in the bottomlands where they could try for the new grass. We moved through them at the purposeful pace Jim had set, and we seemed like a ship with an invisible prow moving through a brown sea that parted before and closed behind us.

Headquarters ranch for the company seemed to my inexperienced eye to be a working ranch of some size. There were barns, huge hay sheds almost empty at this season, two large brush corrals joining a smaller pole one, an oversize wagon shed holding three of the normal ten roundup wagons, and the house itself. All were situated on a bare bench at the convergence of two creeks. Wings of lumber had been added to the original low log building. The sod roofs were already green, the grass roots warmed by the fires inside. A lean-to cookshack had been added to the original wing, which now served as the dining quarters. It was bare and unlovely, with a wheelless buckboard on sawhorses and a grindstone in the front yard.

Dusk was approaching, but the place seemed deserted, although smoke was funneling out the pipe in the kitchen lean-to. We turned our horses into the corral, and Jim led the way to the house. As we approached, a man stepped onto the log sill at the door, and lounged against it. He was a bald man, and wore a dirty undershirt that matched his flour-sacking apron. He was sucking a match, and he spoke around it.

"Howdy, Jim." He nodded to me.

"Where's everybody?" Jim asked.

"Buryin' Meade," the cook said, watching Jim's face, waiting for his next question. But haste was upon him, and before Jim's face could reflect surprise, the cook blurted out the story. Meade Saunders, one of the hands, had been killed by an Indian fence cutter. That was yesterday. Today, they had buried him.

"When?" Jim cut in.

The cook protruded his jaw, using it for a pointer. "This afternoon. Off yonder, about a mile."

"That was this afternoon. Where are they now?"

"They aimed to pay a call on that Cheyenne camp at Willow Springs tonight," the cook said.

Jim said sharply, "Then don't stand there! Get a horse!" He turned and began to run for the corral. Half way there, he turned to call to me. "Stay here, Joey," and I came to a reluctant halt.

I tramped back to the house, and in a few moments they left the place, their horses at a dead run, the cook still wearing his dirty singlet and no coat.

Behind my own excitement was a strange resentment at Jim. He hadn't asked a single question about the death of one of his men; he seemed only concerned with stopping the crew before it took a natural enough revenge. Murdo's prediction that something was "building up" had been right enough. And I remembered Mr. Edmonds' conversation in his office in Reno. Was Santee Paddock behind any of this? Meade's killer and Murdo's attacker had both been Indians, and the Indians had enough grievances, real and fancied, against the whites that it would be hard to tell where their own inclinations left off and Santee's influence began.

I got a supper of sorts on the big iron range in the kitchen, and then went on through it to the bunkhouse. It was a barn of a place, its walls lined with bunks and festooned with worn clothes, its dirt floor littered with leather cuttings and old gloves and worn-out socks and old magazines. Under the kerosene lamp hanging over the big scarred-top table, I found a pack of greasy cards, and I played solitaire far into the night, my ear cocked for the return of the crew. Long after midnight, dead tired, I rolled into one of the bunks in my clothes.

It must have been close to dawn when voices awakened me. It was the crew coming into the bunkhouse. I had slept so soundly that I did not even hear the approach of their horses, and now I roused to see grim-faced men filing into the room and scattering to their bunks, where they sat. Jim came in then, his step quick, his face angry, and behind him was a middle-aged man in a cotton shirt who looked fully as angry as Jim.

In curt tones Jim asked for paper and ink and a pen, and the cook, wearing my slicker over his undershirt against the coolness of the night, said he would get them. Nobody talked, and the men were avoiding Jim's eye. He stood there in the middle of the room, his face stiff, and I knew there was wrath boiling inside him.

When the writing implements came, Jim swept my cards aside, sat down on the bench and announced, "Now how many want to quit? I'll make a draft on Edmonds Brothers for your time and you can clear out."

He looked about the room, and so did I. These fifteen men were all under middle age, and some were young. Their clothes were worn to all degrees of patched shapelessness, the majority of them needed barbering, and some were out at their boots, but there was a kind of iron-hard capability and pride in their quiet manner. Right now, they avoided Jim's gaze and looked at one another or at their cigarets.

"Well?" Jim demanded harshly.

After a short pause, one man said, "I said I would, but I don't reckon I will."

"What about you, Isom?" Jim demanded of the black-haired man standing by me. He moved his body, like a horse shifting his weight to the other hip and said, "Me neither."

Jim shuttled his gaze to the middle-aged man in the checked shirt who lounged against the door jamb, a cigaret cupped in his rough hand. He was the oldest man in the room, and by the way the crew kept looking at him, I knew he was the foreman. I knew, too, that Jim was blaming him for all that had happened, but that even in his anger he had the wisdom not to embarrass the foreman in front of his men. This man said quietly, "I'd like to ask somethin', Jim."

Jim barely nodded, still watching him.

"I can take all this name-callin'," the foreman said steadily. "Now you tell me, so's the crew can hear it. Are we runnin' a shootin'-gallery for Indians here, or is a man allowed to fight for his friends?"

A murmur of assent came from the men. Jim said, "I'll let Isom answer that." He shifted his gaze to the black-haired man. "Isom, who shot Meade?"

"A Cheyenne, I told you."

"What Cheyenne?"

There was a moment of dragging silence, and

then Isom said, "I dunno. We was patching a hole they'd cut in the fence, when the two shots came. Meade went down and my horse went wild and I seen that Indian hightail it."

"What Indian?" Jim insisted.

"I told you, I don't know," Isom said, his voice rising a little.

Jim shuttled his hot gaze back to the foreman. "There you are, Pete-Keach, Isom doesn't know the man. You don't know him. Still, you'll ride into a Cheyenne camp and shoot it up and kill somebody, just to square things."

"How else you goin' to square it?" a man asked.

"Not by killin' innocent men," Jim said flatly, turning to face the man. "Those Cheyennes were punishin' their killers a long time before the white men come here, Barney. They still know how."

"But will they?" Pete-Keach asked drily.

"If they don't, I will," Jim said quickly, flatly. "There'll be one dead Indian to pay for Meade Saunders' death, I can promise you that."

"Then what's the difference between us doin' it and you, or the agent or the army?" Isom said.

"The difference is called justice," Jim said levelly. His glance touched the face of every man in the room. "When we took this lease the War Department said we couldn't expect help from it if the Indians made trouble. These Indians know it. We're outnumbered three hundred to one, so they could have massacred us a long time ago if they took the notion. Then why haven't they? Because we've paid our grass money on time and minded our own business. Then give them a chance to mind theirs, before we take it over."

Jim ceased talking and there was dead silence, then, "It just comes down to money, Isom. There ain't any more to say."

It was a young man's speech, and Jim's glance sought out the speaker. He was about my age, and his face was unnecessarily defiant. I could almost see Jim check the impulse to annihilate his argument with a savage attack. Instead, he smiled, and I was proud of him for that.

"Of course it comes down to money, Kerman. That's why I'm here and you're here and I'm payin' you forty-five a month instead of a trail-hand's thirty, with you doin' less work. I told you what to expect." His glance shifted to take in the whole crew. "I'll tell you again, too. You're bein' paid better money to take a risk. I'll still pay off any man that speaks up."

He waited a long moment, and when nobody spoke up, he went out. The men didn't talk immediately; they moved about doing small things, and I suddenly realized that as long as I remained they wouldn't talk.

I rose and went out into the night. I heard Jim knocking out his pipe on his boot heel, and I turned toward the sound. When I got to the wheelless buckboard where he had been sitting, he was gone. I believe now he heard me coming and left, and he did it for one reason. He was putting my loyalty to the same test as the crew's, and with the same bitter facts to swallow.

Next morning things were quiet at breakfast, but none asked Jim for his time. They split up after breakfast for the day's work, but the affair was not finished. Their very manner proclaimed that they had suspended judgment on Jim until they saw whether or not Meade Saunders' death was avenged, and if it was not they would quit, to a man. Jim knew it, too, I could tell.

We left for Fort Reno at midday, and Isom was with us, for Jim was going to lay the facts of Meade's murder before Agent Coe, with Isom as a witness. This business was riding Jim. He talked little that afternoon and even less in camp that night.

The morning broke windy, with high clouds shredded over a clean sky. Their shadows raced past us, scudding across the tilted prairie in ponderous haste. It was around midday when we had dismounted to drink that Jim, kneeling beside the stream, wiped his mouth and raised his face to the sky.

"I've smelled smoke for an hour," he announced. "Who else has?"

"I have," Isom said.

We pushed on and now I noticed that Jim talked even less and was studying the horizon. Sloping into a swale beyond which was a sharp rise of ground, I dismounted to tighten my cinch, which I had failed to do thoroughly at the creek. Jim and Isom rode onto the rise of ground and stopped. When I caught up with them Jim said to me. "There's smoke to the southeast, Joey. We'll have a look."

I could see nothing at first but Jim pointed out a faint haze there which shadowed the horizon sky. Our pace was faster now and even I could smell the smoke. As we rode on, the smell became more distinct; a thin fog half-veiled the sun and there was a tinge of blue in the hollows as we rode through them. An hour later the smoke had thrown a distinct mud-colored barrier between us and the sun. Jim cut north again to get out of the smoke which was making us cough. There was a definite line visible now where it ribboned out to give us cleaner air, and Jim rode just outside this line, his horse at a fast trot. Already, uneasy cattle stampeded away from our approach.

The land suddenly tilted up to a long low

ridge, and Jim achieved the top first. I saw him suddenly wheel his horse so sharply it reared, and at the same time reach to unbutton the flap of his holster. We met him and before we could get a glimpse of what was beyond the ridge he said, "There's four men down there, Isom. Joey, you stay here." He pulled his horse around and spurred him over to the ridge. Isom, hauling his carbine out of the saddle scabbard, followed, and I trailed Isom.

The first thing I saw was a new fire a quarter mile to the south. Ahead of us and beyond the ridge was a dry creek bottom bare of trees except for a growth of willows. Two men were riding side by side due north on the valley floor. The other two, a hundred yards behind them, were dismounted, watching the flames from a heap of brush they had just touched off.

Without a word, Isom chose the two mounted men and Jim swerved toward the two on foot, perhaps five hundred yards away. Knowing I would be useless, because I was not armed, I tried to anticipate what would happen, but before I could guess the flat sharp crack of Isom's rifle exploded things.

On the heel of Isom's shot the rider closest to us rose up in his stirrups and drove into his partner, whose horse immediately stampeded. The man fell out of the saddle, and his partner pulled his horse around in a wide circle and cut up the opposite slope headed south. Isom shot again, but the man had too much head start. He was half turned in his saddle now, shooting at Isom with a six-gun. I saw too late that I had missed a chance to cut him off, but I put the spurs to my horse and raced down the slope to make a try.

The deeper roar of Jim's six-shooter cut in on Isom's next shot, and I looked for Jim. One of the grass-firers had gained his horse and was streaking south along the willows, low over his horse's neck.

Jim's second shot had hit the grounded man. His leg dragged and he was fighting savagely to get on his frightened horse which was rearing and plunging away from him. Finally, seeing Jim bearing down on him, the wounded man let go the reins and I saw him swing up a six-shooter at Jim.

He had time for two quick shots and then Jim was on him. I saw Jim's hand, holding a gun, rise high over his head. And then he was on the man, and his hand flashed down as he thundered by him. There was a brief instant in which Jim's driving horse hid the man afoot, and then Jim was clear of him. The man was on the ground, and already Jim was angling up the hill to cut off the man I was supposed to be after. I waited an agonizing ten seconds for Jim to roll out of the saddle and when he did not I spurred after him. He and Isom vanished over the ridge, but by the time I had reached it they were trotting back toward me.

Jim was talking swiftly, harshly to Isom as I approached, and he did not look at me. "Get the fence crew, too," he was saying. "Grub for thirty men for a week, tell the cook. Roust out anything on wheels and get all the barrels and tubs you can lay hands on. We'll make our stand back there at the creek where we drank. Get blankets, tow-sacks, tarps — anything that will soak water." He turned to me, his face hard and intent. "Joey, give Isom your horse."

I dismounted and Isom took my fresher horse and rode off at a fast trot. I stepped into the saddle of his horse and Jim pulled over to me and said, "Follow me, Joey. When we run across a steer I want you to help me turn him and drive him back to the fire."

We cut off north at a gallop and Jim's head was turned to regard the fire in the hollow. Since we had first seen it, the fire had spread out in a black fan whose edge plumed up a gray-brown smoke that was soon caught in the slow wind. Tongues of fire, invisible in the sunlight, ate at the dry winter-cured grass, crawling steadily up the slope. Beyond, to the south, as far as sight could reach was the lazy moil of dirty smoke that lifted high and spread and smeared out and drifted west.

We found three steers several hundred yards up the valley, and by separating and coming up ahead of them, we turned them back toward the fire.

Approaching the smoke, Jim put his horse into a run and singled out a medium-sized steer, who stampeded at Jim's approach. Jim's horse easily pulled alongside the steer and then Jim shot. The steer went down, skidding on its side and turned over.

When I caught up with Jim he was dismounted and was severing the head of the steer from its neck. Then he slit the steer's belly from neck to tail.

"Shake out Isom's rope," he ordered me. When I had, he took it, made a half hitch around the steer's hind leg and did the same with his own rope on the other leg. We mounted then and dragged the steer to the edge of the fire, where Jim rolled the carcass over on its split belly.

"You take the side that's burned out, Joey, and I'll ride in the grass. Keep even with me. We're goin' to pull until the steer is split flat, guts down, then drag him over the fire."

Our horses worked furiously, but within half an hour of dragging the split steer back and forth along the edge of the burning grass, Jim choking with smoke, my horse plunging uneasily on the hot ashes, we had that one fire extinguished. The other fires, dozens perhaps, or maybe one big fire now, still smoked to the south.

Only then did Jim, his face shadowed with smoke grime and his hands and clothes caked with blood, ride over to the two dead men. I hung back, sickened and weary, my lungs raw, almost afraid to talk. He had worked with a quiet stubbornness, but his eyes, red-rimmed and bloodshot, were smouldering with an anger that was half-frightening.

He called over his shoulder, "Come take a look, Joey, I want you to remember these faces."

Reluctantly, I followed him. The man he had downed was a white man, a slack-mouthed, unshaven man of medium size dressed in filthy denim pants and utterly shabby in death. His head was turned on one side, hiding the place where his skull was bashed in. I glanced covertly at Jim, my stomach queasy and all anger gone from me, but his expression was hard and thoughtful and obsessed. The other man was a full-blooded Cheyenne in white man's clothes. His face in repose was young and bigoted. Jim dismounted by his side and rolled him over, looking searchingly at his face.

He said quietly, "That's Stone Bull's son, Joey."

"A chief's son?"

Jim raised his glance to me and nodded.

"That squares Meade's killing."

He rose and went back to look at the white man again, and I watched him. He studied that face for a long moment, and then he looked off to the south again, at the slow banners of smoke. I knew his thoughts. The fire was burning the many long miles to our fence, some fifteen miles distant, eating hourly deeper into our range, burning forage and trapping cattle, a grim black desert on the march. And this man at his feet had done it.

There was no pity, no remorse, only a kind of implacable cold anger in Jim's face when he came to the horses and mounted.

"What are we going to do with them, Jim?" I asked.

"Leave them. They'll be after them."

"The white man, too?"

Jim turned his head to look at the man, and then said softly, "Yeah, I got a notion they'll be after him, too."

I remembered Jim's pledge to his men last night — an eye for an eye and a tooth for a tooth — and I understood that I had witnessed a rough justice, the kind these men understood better than any the courts could deal out, and Jim Wade had delivered it.

Afterward, we rode away toward the south to see what the fire was doing. Two of us could not fight it; we had to wait upon every man the company could muster.

We rode over a black, acrid smelling landscape that was in ruin. In the creek bottoms the brush and dead timber were still smoking. Small whirlwinds of gray ashes played along the ridges. We found one band of cattle, a dozen in number, which had sought a plum thicket for protection and were trapped there by the flames. A stink of burned hair and roasted flesh had already drawn a coyote who slunk away at our approach. He had somehow survived the fire and was the only living thing we saw in that afternoon's ride. The fire had touched everything, even the swampy bottomlands where the green grass was already high. The old grass had passed on the flame everywhere, under trees where there were fallen leaves to burn, across sloughs, into thickets of cottonwood saplings, across sandy stretches of buffalo grass, over limestone outcroppings and into the blackjack forests.

We skirted the fire late in the day and rode for the creek, arriving far after dark. Some time in the night the crew started to drift in with spring wagons, buckboards, roundup wagons and freight wagons borrowed from the fence freighters. The cook set up the chuck wagon and near by a rope corral was fashioned for the *remuda*.

With forty men on hand Jim started to work

immediately. He intended to backfire now, making his stand on the west side of the creek. With water close, with men enough to handle it, he could fire a lane on the east bank of the creek running south. If luck held and a higher wind did not rise he might be able to finish the lane before the fire reached the creek.

All that night and through the day the men worked down the creek, and still there was no sight of the approaching fire, only the ominous smoke. We were split up in five crews and each crew assigned two wagons, barrels and blankets. The backfire was started east of the creek, and as it reached the creek and jumped it toward the slope several hundred yards to the west, we assaulted it. Working like mad, choked with smoke, we beat it out with wet blankets. At first it forced us back over the ridge and onto the prairie, but slowly we gained the upper hand and extinguished it. Then we moved the wagons onto the head of the line and repeated the process. Once — I think it was during the second night when the lazy approach of the fire was visible — a fire of our own setting got out of hand, and it took the whole crew to extinguish it. No one thought of sleep. We worked until we were exhausted and then ate and worked some more, burning our way south. There were blistered hands and faces, burned clothes and boots, singed hair and eyebrows. Toward the end of that day we were working in a fog of smoke that had our throats and lungs raw. We could hardly have told night from day, even if we wanted to.

When we reached the fence, what we hoped would be our limit, we found that the fire had crossed over onto land not our own, but unless we fought it there was the chance that it would double back on us. The creek turned sharply east, and we had to backfire trusting to wind and not water. We dropped back miles from the fire then, since we did not care about this range, and started our backfire. Sometimes we went eight hours without food before the harried cook and his chuck wagon could reach us.

It was night when the real grass fire finally reached the backfire. It approached unevenly and when it was upon us, it struck in ragged peninsulas of flame. Clouds of smoke folded skyward, their bellies orange with the reflection of the fire, and a multitude of animal life — rabbits, field mice, baby quail and prairie dogs — scurried in front of it, passing blindly through our waiting line. Night hawks hovered overhead just under the blanket of smoke, and they dived continually for the insects the fire had flushed. When it reached the creek bottom the flames grew hotter, feeding on the brush. Pennants of sparks were carried up and over our heads by the hot draft. Some of them jumped the fire lane and the creek and it was this we had to watch out for. Soaked blankets were the weapons we used. Then at the very peak of its fury the fire would die suddenly and we would rush to a new point.

Three times news came from other crews that the fire had jumped the backfire and the creek. Wearily, each time, we would mount and ride for the place and find that the fire had eaten deep into the prairie and far to the west of the creek water. These times the fire was fought with butchered steers. The men dragged them back and forth until their fireblackened entrails tore loose, and then the riders dropped out for another steer. Only when the tide of the fight was against us was there enough light to see by. When we were winning it was a semi-gloom of choking, pink tinted smoke where horses and shouting riders appeared suddenly in a moment of violent action to disappear just as suddenly.

I lost track of time, and all I could think of was sleep. Already, it had conquered some of us. One man fell off his horse and was sleeping there in the prairie grass in the path of the fire. It was Jim Wade on his ceaseless patrol who found him. The only time Jim was off a horse was when he was lending a hand with blankets. His face was gaunt, his eyes puffed slits in his face, but he was tireless, driving his men until they cursed him. But at the last, when exhaustion conquered and even the cook lay sprawled in the wagon bed asleep, a wet tow-sack in his hand, it was Jim Wade with a handful of the more hardy cowboys, who patrolled the fire lane and fought the last fire out.

I remember I woke up to a noon sky, clear and cloudless. I had no memory of climbing into this spring wagon, and I rose stiffly to look around me. On the grass, in wagons, with and without blankets, men were sleeping. Off to the right behind a roundup wagon, a man was unsaddling the last of the horses. I rose stiffly, my blistered hands aching, and stumbled down out of the wagon bed. The man was Jim Wade, and he walked over to the small fire by the chuck wagon. A cut of ribs was propped up on a stick facing the fire and Jim squatted by it, turning it over. A ranch dog was prowling out on the prairie, nosing at the blackened corpses of the steers. The prairie to the west was greener than I remembered it and a west wind, blessed west wind, was pressing down the tall grass as it passed over.

Jim heard me and turned his head and then he smiled. All the worry and excitement that had been riding him seemed drained from his face, leaving only a tired friendliness.

"Haven't you slept?" I asked.

"I was hungry."

"Is it out?"

He nodded. "The change in wind saved us. Down by the red stone outcrop it jumped us and I thought we had it to do all over again. Then the wind changed."

He shared the ribs with me and I sat so I could look over the east at the blackened landscape. "How much did we lose, Jim?"

He shrugged. "Fifty, seventy thousand acres, maybe." He wrenched off a bite of meat and chewed it patiently. His face was soot-smeared, even patches of his beard-stubble singed. His shirt was in tatters, and underneath I could see the livid welts of numerous burns.

He laughed suddenly. "That's once more we didn't ask the army to help us out."

Midway through his crude breakfast, he rose, swayed a little and said, grinning, "Good night, Joey – or good noon." He stumbled over to the wagon where I had been sleeping and fell into it.

All through the afternoon members of the crew joined the circle around the fire. The cook was at work once more, and a holiday spirit prevailed. Stragglers from the other camps rode in. There was not enough soap to go around, but we tried to wash anyway. All the reserve that had marked these men at the headquarters ranch was gone. They didn't say it, but I knew they felt that the honor of the outfit had been redeemed by Jim and Isom. Two grass-firers were dead, and Meade Saunders was avenged. Thirty men among four thousand Indians, they could still talk to the Indian in the language he respected most, which was with a gun.

Jim was awake for supper and he counted off the crews to repair fence, which had undoubtedly been cut; another was detailed to freight out the half-dozen plows we would buy at the agency to cut fire lanes in case the Cheyennes did not heed the warning of the two dead men. The men joked with him, as one of themselves, and things were right.

Five

In Fort Reno we learned that the news of the grass fire and the killing had preceded us, and that nobody was surprised. The Indians were daily growing bolder, and if the situation during the past winter was bad it was rapidly becoming worse. There were ominous mutterings around the Cheyenne campfires beyond the agency; Cheyenne and Arapaho children had been withdrawn from the agency school, and demands for increased rations had passed the bounds of insolence. Few whites fared abroad at night, and all day long the sullen Indians prowled the streets of the agency, and their mood was increasingly ugly.

Agent Coe told us all this in the settling twilight of his parlor that afternoon, where Jim and Isom and I had come to report the grass fire and the killings as soon as we reached Reno. His mild face had never looked more harried as he told us that his appeals for more troops (he had asked six separate times) had been ignored.

"Mark my words, we're in for a massacre," he finished gloomily.

Jim had listened to Coe's gloomings with patience, but now it melted. "Don't talk like a fool, Coe," he said sharply.

An injured expression crept into Coe's face.

Jim went on bluntly, "You have several hundred Cheyenne and Arapaho children in schools in the East, haven't you?"

Coe nodded.

"If they aren't hostages, what are they?"

Distaste crept into Coe's face. "You are asking that I use that as a threat?"

Jim smiled thinly, "That's Indian language, Coe, the kind they understand. You better learn to talk it." He paused, and I saw his body shift in the dark of the room, and then his voice came bluntly again. "And when you've learned to use your voice, start learning to use your eyes."

Isom, sitting on the sofa beside me, dragged his boot across the rug.

"What's that?" Coe said. "Use my eyes, you say?"

Jim rose slowly. "I told you there were two men killed by us, one an Indian, one a white man. Find out about that white man, and when you understand why he was there, you'll understand a lot more about your Indians."

"Who was that man?" Coe said sharply.

"You're the agent," Jim said strangely. "Find out."

We left then and rode out of Darlington on our tired horses to the garrison. Jim's last words had been as strange to me as they had been to Coe, and I tried to remember what Jim had said that day when he knelt by the man he had killed. And still I didn't understand.

We turned our horses over to the hostler in the dark wagon yard at Edmonds Brothers and climbed the steps and walked down the porch to the saloon door. Jim, in the lead, was just about to open the door, and then he stepped aside.

Santee Paddock stepped through the doorway onto the porch. He was wearing a shapeless black suit that hung awry on his big frame, and the ever present cigar was in his mouth. When he saw the three of us standing there silently, he looked at us carefully, something like slow alarm stirring in his hooded eyes, and then he said affably, "Evening, gentlemen."

"Howdy, Santee," Jim drawled. "Met an old friend of yours a couple of days back."

Santee paused before Jim, his long face bland as butter under the thin light from the street lamp. Isom stepped aside and leaned against the side of the building, away from me.

"That so?" Santee observed, his voice colorless.

"Hughie Dysart. Remember him?"

"Oh, yes," Santee murmured. "Poor Hughie. Went to seed."

"He always was seed."

Jim and Santee regarded each other with a veiled and hard attention.

Then Santee said, "Yes, I guess he was. I wish you'd told me that before he stole fifty head of beef from me."

"Oh, he's not working for you any more?" Jim murmured.

"Hasn't been for two months."

"Or two days. Which?"

Santee was mystified, judging by his attentive frown. But his eyes had never lost that opaque careful expression. "What are you trying to tell me?" he asked slowly.

"Hughie is dead. Shot. By me."

There was a long, still pause. "What for?" Santee asked.

"He set a grass fire."

Santee's face slowly settled into its blandness again. He said softly. "You aren't a very careful man about what you say."

"Pretty careful."

Santee's feet shifted. "When you think you've got proof that Dysart worked for me, look me up."

"If I do get the proof, I won't need your invitation," Jim murmured.

107

Santee turned and walked down the steps. Jim stood there, looking at his back until he was lost in the darkness, and then without speaking to us he walked into the saloon. I looked at Isom. Isom took off his hat and wiped his brow with his shirtsleeve and then followed Jim into the saloon.

My unasked questions were answered now. Santee had been behind the grass fire, perhaps behind Meade's murder and the attack on Murdo. If Jim ever got the proof of Santee's guilt, I knew he would kill Santee. I found my forehead was sweating, too.

A late session with Tom Wynant, during which I fell asleep, brought me down to a late and solitary breakfast next morning after the first night's sleep in a bed since I had left the Ketros' in Texas. Mr. Edmonds brought me a note and a letter from Elizabeth, which I opened first. It had reached Fort Reno soon after I left months ago, and I thought of the few letters I had written her from Texas, and wondered if they had ever reached her. The letter was full of commiseration, and it held a faint irritation for me. She simply didn't understand what I had been doing. The only real information it contained was that she was so well now that she had decided to go back to school again. I tried hard, reading the letter, to recapture my old feeling for her, and I could not. I gave it up, and turned to the note.

It was from Captain Preftake and asked me to see him at the Adjutant's building at my convenience. Elizabeth was forgotten immediately. I reread the note with the fatalism of a man discovering he cannot shake his conscience; for, far from forgetting that Fort Reno held Ellen Preftake waiting for Jim Wade, it had been in the back of my mind constantly. And now here was a note from Captain Douglas Preftake. Had he suspected Ellen and Jim, and was he going to ask me about Ellen, and if he did what was I going to say? My breakfast was spoiled. I ate, hurriedly, to emerge into the warm spring sunshine and walked across to the Adjutant's office, too preoccupied to notice that it was a beautiful day. The Adjutant's building held the offices of the garrison, and I was directed to Captain Preftake.

He welcomed me as a friend and we sat down to discuss the fire, the drovers' business and the eternal Indian situation; and all the time I was searching his square, impassive face for a sign of what was to come. When it did come, I almost laughed.

"Joey," he said finally, "things have been pretty dreary around here lately. We've been afraid to move about much, on account of the Indian scare. But this morning the Cheyenne and Arapaho are holding a Sun Dance at the northern Cheyenne camp. Every blasted one of them will be there." He hesitated, then said diffidently, "I wondered if you'd ride with Ellen? She's been confined to quarters, so to speak, too long. She needs to see new faces."

He misinterpreted my silence; it was the silence of relief, not misunderstanding.

"Not to the dance," he explained. "The Indians will all be at the dance. Just a horseback ride — anywhere."

I found my tongue and said, "Of course. I'd be glad to, Captain Preftake, and the pleasure is all selfish." I was a little surprised at my own gallantry, and Captain Preftake smiled.

"I'm a pretty dull husband, Joey, and the army is dull business." He grimaced a little, and then, as if ashamed of having said it, he rose and said he would send an orderly to tell her to get ready, and I was dismissed.

Later, I wondered why I volunteered so cheerfully, and put it down to the fact that it was because I was so relieved at escaping uncomfortable questioning. For I remembered my resolve of last winter to have nothing to do with such a woman. My hostility was blunted by time, however, and while I was saddling my horse in the wagon yard, I found myself looking forward to the ride with pleasure. I had not been hypocritical to

Captain Preftake in that respect.

Ellen Preftake was waiting for me before their house. Long before I could make out her face she waved to me. When I dismounted and shook hands with her, it was as if everything I had ever thought about her was wiped out of my memory and, as the night when I first saw her, I thought I had never looked upon a lovelier woman. I know now and I knew then why I thought that; it was because she was so fresh looking, as if some magic had created her only minutes before, and nothing had had time to soil her. That night at the german I had thought her skin was almost translucent, a covering that barely hid the glow of life in her, and I had put it down to the kindliness of the lights. But that glow was there now, and against the gray color of her serge riding habit and the blackness of her flat-brimmed low-crowned hat her face was radiant and fresh and alive. There was real welcome in her eyes, too, and I was flattered.

"Joey, you are a bigger man," she said, standing away from me. "Your shoulders are immense. And what happened to that nice office complexion? And the crease in your trousers?"

I laughed and said, "Whatever I am, I owe to horses. Lots of horses."

She laughed too, and I was completely won again. "And now I'm putting you back on one.

111

You're too polite, Joey. You didn't have to go."

"But I wanted to." And I believed I did.

I handed her into the saddle, a side saddle. Before we were out of the barracks square she had me talking about myself, what I had done, what I had learned, and about the trail prospects this year. I considered her questions carefully, wondering if she was trying to lead me around to talking about Jim. But she was not, and then I experienced my first doubts. Maybe she had forgotten about Jim, and he about her. In a way, I almost hoped she hadn't, for then she wouldn't seem so wanton.

We rode north across the rolling prairie, and Ellen seemed to know the country. She said there was a motte of liveoaks and plums ahead that was a pretty sight, although she was afraid the plums were past blossom. Her talk was gay and animated, mostly garrison gossip, and I put it down to the fact that she was glad to be out of the post. Presently we topped a rise that dipped beyond to the liveoaks, and on the fringe of the timber far ahead I saw a tethered horse. A man was sitting beside it, and at sight of us he rose. There was something immediately familiar about the man, though at this distance I couldn't recognize him. But a few yards farther I thought I did, and I said sharply to Ellen, "Isn't that Jim?"

"Yes," she answered, not even looking at me.

She was watching Jim, and there was excitement and softness and delight in her face. I knew then that this meeting had been planned, and that I had been used shamelessly. A disgust with the whole shabby business stirred an anger in me that almost choked me.

I left her, wheeled my horse, and went back up the hill, cursing myself and Jim Wade, and hating him.

Once over the rise I rose in my stirrups and my horse stretched into a run. A minute later Jim rode up beside me and reached out and grasped my horse's bridle, and our horses came to a sliding halt on the grass.

My voice was shrill with anger as I turned in my saddle to face Jim. "Damn you, let me go!"

Jim said quietly, "Turn around, Joey."

"And help you steal a man's wife? To hell with you, Jim Wade! To hell with you!" I rowelled my horse and he reared and Jim pulled aside and I put my horse into a gallop, more furious than ever.

What happened next isn't very clear. I can't say I heard it, but I suddenly felt a rope settle around my body. There was a vicious yank that rammed my elbows against my ribs, my horse simply ran out from under me, and I fell on my side in the tall grass, all the breath driven from me. When I could crawl to my feet, gagging for breath, and claw out of the loose rope, I saw

Jim riding up with my caught horse. He stopped a few feet from me, and his face was calm, hard, unmerciful.

"I didn't want to do that, Joey, but you crowd a man so," he said quietly.

"I'm surprised you didn't shoot at me," I answered bitterly.

Jim only rode up and offered me the reins of my horse. I backed away, putting my hands behind my back and said stubbornly, "If I get on him, I'll ride back to the post."

Jim's face softened a little but not enough to smile. There were still the marks of burns on his face, and one eyebrow was almost gone. It gave him an expression of quizzical tolerance, and from my place on the grass he looked adamant and tough and patient as an Indian. He dropped his reins and mine, dismounted, and walked over to pick up his rope which he had cast loose from his saddle horn. Coiling it slowly, he said in a placid voice, "Joey, you started bein' my conscience for me, back there in Texas. Ellen and I have got to settle this. You wouldn't have brought her if I asked you. Now you've got to stay to make it look right."

"So you're thinking of her reputation now?" I asked hotly.

Jim shook his head. "No, you are," he said quietly. It was the truth, and my glance avoided his. I was still angry, but not so angry that I

114

didn't see the sense in what he said. If I left them now, it would be with the memory of that rapt look in Ellen Preftake's eyes, and the knowledge that they were alone. If I stayed, nothing would be hidden from me. I hated Jim for his shrewdness, then, but I knew I was going to stay, even though it was a despicable blackmail.

Surlily, I mounted and we rode back to the ridge and down the slope. Ellen was sitting where I first saw Jim. We rode up and dismounted, and Jim walked up to Ellen. "Joey wants to say something, Ellen," he said in a matter-of-fact voice. "He thinks I'm a wife-stealer and you're wanton." His face turned to me. "Now that we understand each other, we might's well leave the horses to the flies and find some shade."

In the brief look Ellen gave me there was neither shame nor anger. She took my arm and we walked into the motte, while Jim led the horses into the shade and tethered them. There was a small seep among the oaks that formed a pool before it trickled back among the trees to vanish. Around it the new grass was short and green and cool-looking, and Ellen sank down on it and leaned against a tree. Jim came up then, and he chose a place beside Ellen, leaving me standing stiffly, hostile and ashamed and wholly unbending.

Jim took off his hat and said wearily, "You got the pulpit, Joey. Get out your curry-comb."

I was still too angry to hear the gentleness in those words and, even more than usual, I was ready to take offense.

"I won't do any combing over, Jim. You said everything for me back there."

Jim looked at Ellen and said patiently, "Then sit down and listen."

"Are you going to make me listen to you make love to a married woman?"

Jim took that, too, and while he looked at me I could see the misery in his eyes.

Ellen said, "Joey, I make love to Jim all the time. When I see him and when I don't, when I think of him and when he's in Texas and I am here." She smiled a little bit. "If you're afraid he'll take me in his arms and tell me I'm a dear woman, he won't. He's done that already, and I believe him and I am content with that."

I felt my face go hot with shame and I said quickly, "Why do you tell me these things? I don't want to hear them."

"Because we hope you're our friend," Ellen said quietly.

"But you haven't any right to say it, not even to a friend!"

Jim said softly, "Why not?"

I was shocked out of my anger then, and it was my training and all I ever believed in that made me answer what I did. "Because Ellen is Douglas Preftake's wife."

Jim said levelly, "We didn't know each other when Ellen married Doug, Joey."

"So a woman takes the first man that comes along if she likes him better than her husband," I said, outraged. "I'm younger than you are, Jim, but I know that won't work."

Jim looked at me a long time, neither shame nor argument in his face, and Ellen's hand presently stole into his. He turned his head a little and smiled faintly, and she smiled back. I had seen my father and mother do that, and knew it for the gesture of two people whose understanding put them beyond need of speech. I discovered something then, something I should have known from the beginning, and I blurted out my question. "Do you want to marry Ellen, Jim?"

"I'm going to."

I sank down on the grass, and I was suddenly filled with a wild and unreasonable gladness. I'd been a prig and a fool, and maybe I still was, but in my own mind now, Ellen wasn't a wanton woman, and Jim wasn't on another conquest. I had my first understanding then of that terrible compulsion of nature Ellen spoke of as love. I understood now why Ellen would sneak away to meet Jim, shedding her conscience like a cloak; now I knew why Jim had never bothered to defend himself in all these months since I accused him. He and Ellen simply wanted to be husband and wife. They were my friends now, utterly and completely, and there were no reservations in my feeling.

And then I remembered Ellen was married, but instead of being outraged at the recollection, now I was dismayed, and for the first time I sensed the futility and desperation that had been riding them for months. The barrier had a new face now, more sobering than the old.

I said to Ellen, "Does Douglas know?"

"Jim won't let me tell him."

"You say you're his friend, Jim," I said.

"I am his friend." He looked away from me and began to pluck grass and throw it aside. "I know what you're thinking, Joey. It isn't honest. I like Doug, only my likin' for him can't keep me from havin' Ellen."

"Then how will you do it?" I asked slowly. "How can you take her without leaving him feeling the way you do now?"

Ellen had been watching Jim, but now she turned to me and spoke with quiet passion, her face radiantly alive. "If you're talking of justice, Joey, then why not consider me? I have been Doug's wife, and a good one! I don't want to be any more, because it's wrong! It's more wrong than going away with Jim!"

"Who will think so?" I asked.

"Jim and I! Maybe you. The only people that count!"

"That's not so," Jim said gently, stubbornly. "Ellen is coming to me as my wife, or not at all. I'll give no cause to humiliate her."

"Oh, Jim, you big fine fool!" Ellen cried. "Do I care? Haven't I spent ten years being a good woman, and having men love me for it? Do you think I would rather have that love than yours?" She looked at me and her mouth was almost bitter. "I know what you think, Joey. But I've earned the right to Jim. I've never complained, even if my life was one stuffy army post after another. I don't even think I should be excused because I married Doug when I was sixteen, and without sense enough to see what I was doing. All that was coming to me, because it was part of my bargain." She leaned toward me now, her fist clenched in the grass, her eyes pleading passionately for understanding. "Oh, don't you see, Joey, it's me, it's time, it's hunger! Half my life is already lived without Jim. I can't wait any longer! Nothing that will ever happen to me with Doug is as precious as being with Jim!"

I had never seen Ellen when she wasn't calm and sure of herself. She was sure of herself now, but she was not calm. It was as if all the easy loveliness of her was peeled off, leaving only a desperate and lonely woman for me to see. I said, partly in awe, "You'd run away with Jim?"

"Today," she said swiftly.

"No!" Jim said sharply. Young as I was, I knew Jim's whole misery then. He wanted Ellen more than life, and yet he would not do a dishonorable thing to get her.

We sat there in dismal silence, each looking at the others. Jim's horse back among the trees nickered loudly, and was answered by an approaching horse.

I jumped to my feet and said, "There's someone coming," and I believe the sense of guilt I felt made me sure it was Captain Preftake approaching. But it wasn't.

Three Indians, Cheyennes, riding single file among the trees, came up to the seep. Obviously, they had come to water their horses, but they checked them now, regarding us in hostile surprise. Their faces were painted and they had reverted to full Indian dress — beaded leggings, necklace of teeth, feathers, vermilion paint and all. They were a savage-looking trio, and later I learned they were the Dog Soldiers sent out to summon the other Indians to the Sun Dance. They talked among themselves in low voices, never taking their glances from us. Presently, one of them, a tall lithe Indian with a hideously painted face that accentuated his natural look of ferocity, slipped off his pony and came around the seep. Jim rose, too, and stepped out in front of me. I remember the puzzled expression on Jim's face when I glanced at him.

When the Indian came closer, Jim said, "How," waiting for the Cheyenne to return his greeting before they shook hands. But the Cheyenne did not answer. He walked over to Ellen and said something in a guttural commanding tone.

Jim spoke in Comanche, and the Cheyenne looked up at him and answered in Cheyenne. Jim listened carefully, and then shook his head, not understanding. The Cheyenne began to make signs, then, and we both came closer to him. The mounted Indians pulled their horses around the end of the seep and were watching from close by.

First, the Cheyenne pointed to Ellen, then to Ellen's hat which was on the ground beside her, then to the seep, made a scooping motion as if holding the hat, and followed it with the gesture of drinking. It was not clear to me if he wanted to borrow Ellen's hat to drink from, or whether he wanted Ellen to give him a drink.

Whichever it was Jim spoke one word sharply, and that in Cheyenne, and it didn't take a knowledge of the language to know that he was saying "No."

The Cheyenne began an angry harangue, and Jim spoke under it to me. "Reach for my gun, Joey, and watch those other two."

I was behind him, and close, and I reached under his coat, opened the flap of his holster and slipped out his heavy six-shooter.

The Indian ceased speaking.

Ellen said, "If it will stop this trouble, Jim, I'll get him a drink."

"Sit where you are," Jim said quietly, staring at the Indian. Then he slowly shook his head in the negative.

The Cheyenne sneered, leaned down and put out his hand toward Ellen's shoulder. I don't think he touched her, because Jim was quicker. His hand came down, smacked on the Indian's wrist, and carried the Indian's arm behind his back with such force that I heard the sickening sound of tearing ligaments just before the Indian screamed. I saw Jim seize him by the breech clout and hair and then lift him entirely above his head and then hurl him pinwheeling into the seep.

I had the wit to wheel, the gun in my hand, and face the two mounted Indians, but I did not look at them. I saw the Cheyenne land head first in the water, and then, his back arched fully, he came to an abrupt stop, for the seep was shallow. He seemed to stand for a moment on his face in the water, his back bent to breaking, and then he toppled over to fall on his front in the shallow water.

I felt the gun roughly swept out of my hand, and I got a glimpse of Jim's face, white and savage with a terrible anger, as he tramped past me down to the two Indians. He spoke one sentence, in Comanche, I think, and it sounded as wicked as a bull whip cracking. The two Indians slid off their horses, splashed into the pool at a run and picked up the prone Cheyenne. They carried him back to his horse, literally threw him over it, then mounted and rode off, one of them holding the hurt man to keep him from sliding off. Their haste was eloquent of their fear.

I heard Ellen breathing beside me, and we were both watching Jim. He holstered his gun, and glanced briefly at us, and then rubbed a hand over his face, turned and came back to us.

He said to us both, then, "I have lived too long in Texas to like that from an Indian."

Ellen was pale, and I was trembling, and it was not from any fear, but from witnessing this violence.

Jim said, "You'd better take Ellen back, Joey," and we started for the horses. Ellen slipped her hand through Jim's arm and we walked back to the horses in silence.

When the time came for Jim to say goodbye to Ellen, he took off his hat and put a hand on her horse's mane. "I have got to think this out," he murmured. "I'll be going out tonight."

Ellen nodded. She brushed her hand lightly over Jim's and smiled, then picked up the reins, while Jim stepped back. That was their meager and stiff goodbye. Before I rode out Jim gave me his gun and said, "Get her back in a hurry, Joey."

I did. Too much had happened for me to want to talk much, and I felt as miserable as Ellen. We parted at her house, and although the day was still bright and the air soft with spring I was as joyless as a mourner. For, though I now loved Ellen Preftake and Jim Wade more than any friends I was ever to make, I knew they were beaten. Jim could fight for her like a lion, as I had just seen him do, and Ellen could offer herself for the taking, but the thing that would stop them lay in Jim Wade's own conscience. I did not then think it curious that, whereas I began this day with suspicion of them, I was now fiercely loyal and wholly sympathetic.

I didn't see Jim again until that night, when he briefly informed me in my room that I was to leave for Caldwell on tomorrow's stage to open the office. While he gave me the number of cattle cars he wanted on certain dates, the arrangements for feeding and shipping, the credits I was to open and the thousand details of my job, there was little about him to remind me of what we had talked of this day. His

124

armor was complete.

Only when we were finished with our business did he let down.

"About that ruckus at the seep, Joey. If it gets out, then the Indians are wrong in saying there were two men there. Only you and Ellen were there."

"That would make me a pretty big man," I said soberly. "You think anyone will believe it?"

"No," Jim said. His voice held a deep discouragement.

I waited a long moment, and then said, "How does it end, Jim? Will you and Ellen leave it like this?"

"It'll end in divorce."

My face must have shown surprise, for this solution hadn't occurred to me. And it must have shown in my face, too, that I didn't like it, for Jim's glance fell away from mine.

"For a divorce, doesn't there have to be a reason?" I asked then.

Jim nodded. "All bad ones, too."

"Will Ellen do that? Get a divorce?"

"She'll do anything," Jim said quietly. "It's me. I don't like it, Joey."

"But if it's the only way, you've got to like it, haven't you?"

He nodded and came out of the chair and picked up his hat. "Some day, I reckon I will."

He looked at me then and said, "Right now, I don't, Joey," and he went out.

I took up my job in Caldwell with some reluctance, for I had lost my taste for office work. Once the place was scrubbed, the inkwells filled, new pen points supplied and the stove removed, I saw that nothing had changed except myself and the weather. Caldwell was the same town, although the Forces for Good had girded their loins and put through an ordinance prohibiting the sale of liquor. The open saloon, bad as it was, had been replaced by the Blind Tiger, which was worse; and the per capita consumption of liquor by the Cherokee Outlet cowboys did not noticeably diminish. The threat of the quarantine law had little effect on the town's business, for the thousands of cattle wintered on the Outlet did not come under the quarantine.

My days were busy, for I was preparing to receive our firm's trail herds. Our commission men in Kansas City were my immediate bosses, keeping me informed of the market, telling me when to have cars ready for shipment. Jim, in Fort Reno, was informed by the commission men through the post telegraph of the number, age and approximate weight of the cattle desired, and the date they must be shipped. Somehow, it all fitted together, each of us working blindly. My train would be made up, and switched to the siding, and there would be the cattle in the pens, having arrived the night before. And as Jim methodically drained the herds off our Indian leases, Mr. Tressel just as methodically filled them up with fresh herds we had bought in Texas. What herds we had contracted for delivery to the Montana and Wyoming army posts and Indian agencies went through Dodge City to the west, and Jim took care of them.

Fifty ranchers in the Cherokee strip were playing the same game as Tressel, Satterfield and Wade, and when the market was good it took influence and drinks and secrecy and bluff to get cars and a loading schedule. Prepared by Jim and Mr. Tressel, I did well enough, but at first I was unsure of myself.

The letters I received from Elizabeth Lowell did little to help my confidence. There were three of them waiting for me when I got to Caldwell, all weeks old, and in all she tried to console me for the misfortune of being sent to Texas, telling me that I was no match for those ruffians. Knowing what I did of Texas, this was absurd. But when her later letters continued in the same strain, they angered me. I was working for and with these same Texans. If you had a decent respect for their quick-triggered pride and did not interfere in their quarrels, they were an easy lot to get along with. Their casually spoken word was more to be respected than the legal contracts of non-Texans, and I, for one, did not sit in judgment of their morals like a Presbyterian elder.

It may have been Elizabeth's letters that made me reluctant to hunt up Mr. Lowell, but Caldwell is small, and I could plead the urgency of getting acquainted with my job only so long before offense was given. When I walked into his store, his greeting was a curious one. I found him in the rear of the place in his neat office, and he regarded my rough clothes, my stockman's boots, my added twenty pounds and my weather-browned face with obvious distaste.

"Well, Joel," he said, rising to offer his soft hand, "have you lived with those roughs so long you've gone native?"

I surprised myself by answering, "You're damned right, Mr. Lowell."

After that, we saw little of each other although I was invited once to the Lowells' for dinner, and they insisted upon getting the details of my journey to Texas. They were appalled at what I told them of frontier Texas, and when I recounted the details of the grass fire and the fight that preceded it, Mrs. Lowell looked politely but definitely pained. Later, when Mr. Lowell and I were alone, he reprimanded me sharply for not sparing Mrs. Lowell the more unpleasant details, although I was not aware that I had discussed them with an unwholesome relish. I couldn't help but wonder what Mrs. Lowell, with her delicate sensibilities, would have done if she had had to watch Jim Wade almost tear the arm off a Cheyenne and then practically break his back for good measure. Ellen Preftake had watched it, and she neither screamed nor fainted, and I had an idea that her sensibilities were more keen, if not more delicate, than Mrs. Lowell's. At any rate, by tacit agreement the Lowells and I saw little of each other thereafter.

The rumors coming up from the Indian Territory were not encouraging. Opinion was that Coe would have a first-class massacre on his hands if things were not remedied this summer. More than ever before, the Indians were levying on the beef of the trail herds. One trail driver who resisted had been shot from ambush. I had to keep remembering Jim's brief statement to Coe the night we reported the grass fire, and I could only hope he was right.

June found me just getting into the swing of my business. One morning I was called out south of town by one of our firm's riders. We were shipping a large herd of triple-wintered beef, the most valuable cattle on our lease. They had been grazed slowly up from the northeast corner of our lease at a rate that would not take off one ounce of their heavy tallow. But little things can happen to a herd, and one of these things is that while bedded down for the night near the stockpens waiting their turn for loading, a blast of a train whistle can stampede them in seven different directions. To remove the chance of a last minute stampede, during which they would run off pounds of tallow, I had arranged with a rancher who lived two miles from Caldwell for permission to water and bed down our valuable herd on his grass. The cattle would arrive there in a few hours, the rider said, where they would rest until time for shipping tomorrow morning. I went with him to help locate them and inform the rancher, and did not get back until late afternoon. With me were a half dozen of the company riders who had been given liberty for the night. My instructions from Jim through the trail boss were to pay these men off on this night, and I did so. Nothing would do but that I have a drink with them at one of our more famous Blind Tigers. I agreed, and when I left them it was past the supper hour. I was hungry as a wolf from my day on horseback, but for fear I would forget the names of those I had paid off I headed for the office to make a note of it.

It was dusk as I climbed the stairs. The door

was unlocked and I stepped into the hot room to find a man sitting in the lone easy chair.

He rose and said something and not until he spoke did I know that it was Captain Preftake. I thanked my luck that he had waited in the half dark instead of lighting the lamp, else he would have seen the unease on my face as we shook hands. By the time I had lighted the lamp, slapped the dust from my hat and my trousers, I had myself in control.

I said, "Wait until I do some writing, Captain, and I'll have my supper with you." I was searching among the books, not looking at him.

He answered, "Thanks, no. I'm in a hurry and I think I'll try to make Pond's station tonight."

An immense relief flooded me, for I did not want to spend the evening in his company, knowing what I did about Ellen. I put the book away and climbed up to my stool facing him, hoping that he only wanted to pay his respects, but wondering how long he had waited here for me.

He was a soldierly looking man as he sat there. His blue tunic was not especially neat, and his worn boots were certainly unpolished, and even the stripe on his trousers was a little frayed. But this heavy face with its full, soft mustache, and mild, steady eyes and his solid presence bespoke a leader and an able soldier.

A scattering of cigar butts at his feet told me his wait had been a long one.

He lighted another cigar and looked around the office and then at his black cavalryman's hat on the chair and finally at his cigar, and then he cleared his throat. He was going to say something important, I could see, and I forestalled him by asking about Ellen. I was told she was fine, and that she sent her regards. I asked about the Indian situation and was informed that it was a little worse than when I left. I didn't persist along this line, however, because small talk obviously was not suiting my visitor's mood.

He cleared his throat again, and this time he said, "Joey, there's something that has been puzzling me for some time. I'd like to get it straight."

I didn't say anything, and hoped I didn't look too wary.

"Major Corning has had me working with the Indians lately, sounding out their grievances with a view to making some concessions." He had his mouth open to continue, and seemed to change his mind. Anyway, he puffed on his cigar a moment and then said mildly, "There's a faction among the Cheyennes that is very hostile to Jim Wade."

"That's pretty common knowledge," I said. "He killed one of that faction, a chief's son, at the grass fire."

"They don't resent that so much. It's something else that happened."

I waited for him to go on.

"A month or so ago," he said slowly, "three Dog Soldiers got in an argument with Jim, and it came to blows. Jim broke this Cheyenne's shoulder, then threw him to the ground. The Indian has not walked since. Internal injuries, I would say." He ceased talking.

Captain Preftake, waiting for my answer, was presenting me with the choice of lying or telling the truth. And I knew with sudden anger that I was not going to lie. My only hope was that the boldness of my reply would kill whatever suspicions he had.

"The Indian deserved it," I said warmly. "He was trying to force Mrs. Preftake to water his horse out of her hat. He tried to lay hands on her."

"Jim told you," Captain Preftake said.

"No," I answered quickly. "I was there and saw it happen, and the blame is on the Indian, not Jim."

I hoped that by crying indignantly against the Indian's claim I could divert him, but Captain Preftake was a stubborn man.

"I'm not concerned about the justice of it," he said slowly. "It's just that I hadn't heard of it." He looked at his cigar. "Didn't it happen the day of the Sun Dance, when I asked you to go riding with Ellen?"

"Yes."

"And Jim went with you?"

I said casually, "No, we met him when we were riding, Captain."

"Why wasn't I told of the quarrel?" he asked, and there was no reproof in his voice. "Neither you nor Ellen nor Jim ever mentioned it."

"Why, Jim left that night for the lease and I left for Caldwell next day. We didn't have much of a chance."

"Then why didn't Ellen?"

I was neatly trapped, and I could feel my face getting hot. "I suppose because she didn't want it to worry you. After all, no harm came to her. She probably didn't want to worry you," I repeated lamely.

Captain Preftake leaned forward in the chair. "Are you sure that's the reason, Joey?"

I said with some heat, "No, I'm not sure, Captain Preftake! Why don't you ask her?"

"I have asked her," he said slowly, carefully. "She denies that Jim Wade was there."

Poor Ellen, I thought. She had lied to her husband, and clumsily, and I wondered why. If she had rushed to her husband and told him that Jim had quarreled with an Indian in her presence, Douglas Preftake would never have wondered at Jim's being there, or if he had he would have accepted any explanation. But we were all innocents at the game of deception, and Ellen was caught up. And looking at Captain Preftake now, seeing the accusation in his eyes, I despised the man, and wholly without reason.

"And you have come to me so you can prove her a liar?" I asked.

"I wanted the truth," he said doggedly.

"You have it. Are you any happier?"

His gaze did not falter, and I believe he did not hear my question. "Joey," he said carefully, "is Jim Wade in love with Ellen?"

I came down off my stool to face him, angry with myself and with him and with all this mess. "I won't answer that!" I cried. "What kind of a man are you to ask it? Talk to her! Talk to Jim!"

I saw contempt come to his eyes, and he said gently, "You have a queer kind of whiskey-guts, haven't you, Joey? You'd arrange a lover's meeting behind my back, but when it's put up to you you shove the blame on a woman."

"You're a liar!" I shouted. "I didn't plan that meeting!"

He didn't move, didn't even seem to be angry. "Never a liar, Joey," he said mildly, "just honestly mistaken. Only, I don't believe I'm mistaken." He came to his feet, reached for his hat, and then regarded me with a kind of pitying contempt. "You're young, Joey, but not so young you have to do the bidding of a man who treats all women like a honkatonk wench."

"If you mean Jim Wade, you're a liar twice over!"

"Good night," he said mildly, and walked out of the office.

I sank down in the easy chair, trembling with anger, smarting under the lash of Captain Preftake's words. I did not blame him for holding me guilty, nor for loathing the shabbiness of it, just as I had loathed it. But where in my eyes Jim and Ellen's need for each other had seemed to excuse what they had done, it would seem only dishonorable to Captain Preftake. It did to me too, now. I put my face in my hands and stared at the floor, trying to estimate the damage my words had done. Through my tale-telling a man's home probably would be broken up, and it did little good to tell myself that I had spoken the truth, because it was still a shabby truth. A remorse came over me that made me almost physically sick. I loathed myself for what I had just done, for it seemed to me that I had purchased a clean conscience at the expense of torment for three people. But gradually a little reason crept into my thinking. Jim and Ellen had no right to place me in a position to hurt them by telling the simple truth, and hurt Captain Preftake, too. Why should I lie to a decent man to hide the love they were afraid to tell him of? In the space of a few minutes, the pendulum had swung back, and now I was cursing Jim's cowardice and Ellen's foolishness. And then I began to doubt again, and remorse returned. It was the most miserable hour I have ever spent sitting in judgment of myself. I had not the wisdom to see it, but my problem was Jim Wade's problem on a tiny scale. But where I already had made my choice, he had not. I could only remember that I had been disloyal to two persons I loved, with my only compensation a smug feeling that I had come out of it without lying.

It was full dark when I came to my feet, my mind made up. I would try to compensate for a measure of what I had done. Mounting the stool and taking pen and paper, I wrote a note:

Dear Jim:

Captain Preftake was in today asking about your fight with the Cheyenne at the Seep. I didn't lie to him but Ellen did and now he knows about you and Ellen. He asked me about that, but I wouldn't tell him. Still, he knows.

I want to quit. I will stay here until you send a man to relieve me.

Very truly y'rs
Joel Hardy.

He could consider that a warning of things to come. As for myself, I was gloomily certain that it was time for me to leave. Ever since the night I had stumbled onto Ellen in Jim's arms at the german, I had, by a series of clumsy blunders, involved myself in their lives. I didn't like what they had done and were doing, yet I liked them. But Jim's refusal to choose his course and Ellen's refusal to make him choose it had delayed any decision until now events had overwhelmed them, and me with them. There was no way I could help them now, so I had better leave before I saw them broken or was forced to help break them.

That same night I took the note out to where our herd was bedded down, and on the pretext that I had an important business communication for Jim, I got the loan of a messenger to deliver the note. Afterward, I waited for the feeling of relief to come at having washed my hands of the whole affair. But it did not come because I knew nothing was changed, and that I was just running away.

After this night I laid into my work with a will, bound that I would not loaf at my job because the end of it was in sight. I couldn't have loafed if I'd wanted to — not for a week, anyway.

And then something happened that was to change everything. The first hint of it was a terse telegram from our commission agents telling me to disregard all previous orders, to cancel requests for cars in excess of a certain number to handle the small herd on the trail now and to await further orders. The telegram caught me at the stock pens in the afternoon.

That evening at the Drover's House I learned there had been a sharp break in the market. Later that night, the Caldwell *Free Press*, hours tardy so as to get the full story, confirmed the rumors that were in all the gambling houses and hotels.

Commissioner of Indian Affairs, Atkins, had asked that all leases on the Cheyenne-Arapaho reservation be cancelled!

He also requested that the Secretary of Interior, Lamar, send more troops to Reno; that the Indians be disarmed and that a new agent be appointed.

But I had no eyes for these last items. I read the part about the leases over and over, scarcely able to believe it. That was why the market had broken. Agent Coe had finally got his troops, but at what cost to us!

Afraid to think about it, I immediately sought the hotel lobbies, where the stockmen gathered. I had made the acquaintance of most of them through my work, and now I asked their opinions. As I listened to them, my fears slowly melted. In the first place, nobody could be sure of anything, they said, because the Interior Department and the War Department had seldom agreed in the past. In the second place, although the government had a right to annul the leases without having to justify itself, the Indians wouldn't stand for the sudden withdrawal of the lease money; it would bring an uprising. All in all, it would be neither good business nor good government. Coe had yelled so long and so loud for help that he had finally waked up the politicians, and now they must have their day. The garrison would be reinforced, the Indians would subside and the cattle business would prosper. Go to bed, Joey, and let the commission agent and receiving houses fight for your welfare. That was how experience spoke, and I did go to bed, convinced that we were in for a slack two weeks and nothing more.

I got the one herd shipped and then sat around in idleness, and that was bad. It gave me time to imagine what had happened at Fort Reno between Jim and Ellen and Captain Preftake. No news came up from Reno, and I wondered if it was because Jim was so disgusted with me that he could not trust himself to write. I was tied to the office through the very lack of orders. Boredom drove me to the law books again, which I read with an ear cocked for footsteps on the stairs. In those hot days of waiting I had plenty of time for regret. I was not only sorry for what I had done, but I even regretted that I had asked for a man to relieve me. I hoped he wouldn't come.

Then Jim Wade came to town. He swung off the caboose of a train from the Dodge City junction, his sacked saddle over his shoulder. I was yarning with the station agent when I caught sight of him, a tall slow-moving man with his hat cuffed back off his forehead, tramping down the cinder right of way with a wadded and sooted handkerchief in his free hand and the same grave impudence in his face. I gave a shout and went to meet him, my fears forgotten. He had come from Dodge City, and "wasn't that a merry hell of a ride," and how was I?

There was nothing about his greeting different from before, and with a sinking feeling I was certain he had not got my note, and that I would have to tell him about it. The fact that he had come on a train from Dodge only made me the more sure of this.

We went up to the office, and Jim sat in the leather chair, quizzically regarding his name in big letters on the door, as if he had never noticed it before.

I couldn't get up the courage to blurt out that I had told Captain Preftake things I shouldn't have, and that I had wanted to quit. The Indian

Commissioner's request was heaven-sent as a topic of conversation. I asked Jim his opinion and he said quietly that he thought all hell was going to bust loose. I opened my eyes; this was not the optimism of the cattlemen here. Jim had been in touch by telegraph with our eastern Senator and Mr. Satterfield, and the facts of the case were grim enough. The complaint had been lodged against our firm in particular.

"By Coe?"

"No. Santee. He's a patient devil, Joey. He hasn't yelled as loud as Coe, but he's yelled longer and in the right tone of voice, I reckon."

Jim had never underrated Santee Paddock, but it was news to me that he had influence in Washington. I had thought of him as a disgruntled frontier beef-contractor, but nothing more. I was mistaken. Allying himself with the Boomer faction in Washington who wanted the Territory opened up for the plow, he had never missed a chance to turn a trick. I listened while Jim said some sort of hearing was likely to be held on the subject of the Indian leases, and that it might be held at Fort Reno. We would welcome a chance to state our case, he said.

And then he added, "Joey, I've got a last favor to ask of you, and no right to ask it. Would you come from St. Louis as a witness in case we need you at the hearing, provided I paid all expenses?"

"So you got my note," I said, embarrassed.

Jim nodded. He was embarrassed too. He got up and walked to the window and with his hands in his pockets he stood with his back to me looking down on the street. I didn't know what to say, or if I should say anything, and Jim didn't speak immediately. When he did it was without turning around.

"Joey, I guess I'm a triflin' man after all. I don't know how to treat a friend, and I don't deserve one. If it would make you feel better, or help change your mind, you can kick me down those stairs." He paused, then added quietly, "It would make me feel better."

I couldn't find my voice for a moment, out of surprise, and then I asked, "Change my mind about what, Jim?"

"Quittin'." He turned slowly, and his expression was almost shy. "If you do, Joey, you'll never be rawhided again on account of Ellen and me."

I spoke what was in my heart then. "Jim, you can't help but hate me for what I did, and Ellen can't either! That's why I want to quit. Oh, damit, Jim, I didn't know what to do when Captain Preftake asked me about it! I did wrong, maybe, but I did it before I knew it!"

"You did right," Jim said softly, vehemently, almost angrily. "Why should you lie for me or for Ellen? And what kind of a man am I to put

143

off on you the tellin' of a man that I'm goin' to take his wife?"

"You should have told him long ago."

"I know that." He came over to face me and he spoke earnestly. "Joey, it's a pretty sorry thing when a man can't face what he's made for himself. I aim to fix that. If you want to stay, you stay."

"I do."

Jim looked at me closely, and then he smiled the same way he did that night at Reno before I left for Caldwell. "God knows *why* you do," he murmured.

I felt like a man reprieved, and I knew then that I was Jim Wade's man whether he was right or wrong, the same way I was Ellen Preftake's. I could even take Captain Preftake's unjust contempt because they were part of my life, the same as I was part of theirs; and I would rather have been miserable working for Jim than happy working for someone else.

We didn't tarry long in Caldwell, for Jim was anxious to get to Reno. While I arranged for horses, Jim hunted up some of the big drovers to compare notes with them. But nothing was being shipped except the stuff that had been contracted far in advance, and nobody knew when the market would strengthen. It was already known that the troops under the Department of the Missouri Command had left for Fort Reno.

When Jim met me at the livery stable, he looked briefly at my horse and at the one I had picked for him, refused them, went out to the corral and chose two short-coupled and ugly mounts, and we changed saddles. We were in a hurry, was his excuse.

There was none of the easy loafing of our trip up from Texas in this ride. We rode all the daylight hours and sometimes into the night to reach a stage station, for we were traveling light, without food or bedding.

We got into Fort Reno on the third night, and it would have been obvious to the most ignorant that something was happening there. The new troops had arrived the day before, and the garrison had a different air, one almost of festivity, for the fear of an Indian uprising had been allayed. As we rode past the porch of Edmonds Brothers' store to the wagon yard, we could see that the two sutlers' bars were thronged. The long porch was filled with cattlemen conversing in small groups.

We unsaddled in the crowded wagon yard, and then, dead tired, mounted the steps to the long porch that would take us to the hotel entrance. But before we were a third of the way down the porch, Jim was besieged by worried groups of stockmen, the smaller lessees around us. They wanted advice. What was the Canadian Cattle Company going to do?

"Tell the truth," Jim told them. "It's our grass money that's fed the Indians and kept them from risin'. We're payin' hard money for grass that would go to seed. The army wants us here, the agency wants us here and the Indians want us here. That's all their investigation will turn up."

Somebody invited Jim to the bar, and suggested they plan their course of action tonight. But Jim refused to discuss business that night, and we got our rooms and went upstairs.

I washed in my own room and then went over to Jim's. He had stripped off his shirt and was lathering his neck and his face when a knock came on the door. I rose from the bed and opened the door, and there stood Captain Preftake. I was so confounded I could not speak and Jim, whose face was lathered, said, "Who is it?"

Captain Preftake stepped past me. "It's Doug, Jim."

Jim was still for a part of a second, and then he said, "Good. I was on my way to your place now. Sit down."

Captain Preftake didn't sit down. He walked to the head of the bed, his glance on Jim, who was quickly drying his face and climbing into his shirt.

I said, "I'll see you at supper, Jim," and put

146

my hand on the doorknob.

Captain Preftake said, "I'd like to talk to you too, Joey."

My impulse was to throw open the door and bolt, and with this in mind I said coldly, "I can't think of anything we have to talk about."

"I think we have," Captain Preftake said grimly. "We had a conversation in Caldwell. I'd like to see if you have guts enough to repeat it here."

The way he was watching me made me forget my exit, and what he said made me forget my resolve to have no further part in this. I walked up to him, my lips stiff with anger, and said, "I've got guts enough to prove you a liar this time, and the facts, too. What do you want to know?"

"Joey," Jim said quietly. I didn't pay any attention to him. I watched Preftake shift his bright hard gaze from me to Jim.

"Joel told me in Caldwell of your meeting with him and Ellen that day you had the trouble with the Cheyennes. He said it wasn't planned."

"I said it wasn't planned by me!" I corrected him.

"It was planned by me and Ellen," Jim said levelly. "Joey didn't know it, or he wouldn't have done it."

"Ellen said it wasn't."

"She lied to you, I reckon," Jim said gently. "She won't any more, now that you know."

"I don't know anything, except that you and my wife arranged to meet behind my back, through Joel and myself." Captain Preftake's voice was thickening with anger.

"That's true," Jim said softly. "You've likely guessed the rest."

"If I have guessed right," Captain Preftake said slowly, "I'll kill you. Are you and —"

"Doug!" The warning in Jim's voice was sharp and urgent and plain, and it rode down Captain Preftake's words, leaving them unfinished.

"You might have guessed that Ellen and I love each other, even if she is still your true wife."

I had often wondered during those past two weeks what had passed between Ellen and Douglas Preftake on his return from Caldwell, and now I had a clue to it. Ellen, confronted with her lie, had refused to talk, and he had tormented himself to a conclusion that was false.

Jim saw it, and a kind of cold contempt crawled into his eyes. "Your *true* wife, I said."

Captain Preftake was a simple man, a literal man. He asked haltingly, "Are you . . . trying to tell me that Ellen loves you, and not me?"

"I am."

I know the only thing that kept Captain Preftake from Jim's throat was the certain knowledge that Jim spoke irrevocable truth. There was a kind of serene and open confidence in the way Jim faced him that no wish, no hope could deny. A taut silence ran on in the room, while Doug, his bright unbending attention searching Jim's face, stood utterly still.

"I don't believe it," he said at last.

"You do believe it. You know it."

Captain Preftake's stubborn gaze held to Jim's. "If it's true, what are you going to do?"

"Wait."

"For what?"

"Until you give her a divorce," Jim said quietly.

Captain Preftake's face showed an astonishment behind his answer, and he shook his head, as if he could not believe what his ears had heard. He said, then: "You think I'd do that to accommodate you?"

"No. I think you'll do it because the only thing you want is to make Ellen happy. That's the only way you can, ever."

Jim had taken brutal and merciless advantage of him. What he had said was true, and the three of us knew it.

Jim repeated then, "I'll wait."

There was no answer from Captain Preftake;

he looked bleakly, helplessly at Jim for a full five seconds, then he turned and saw me. Slowly, a kind of exhausted sanity came back into his eyes, and he frowned, as if trying to recall something. Finally, he succeeded. "I did you an injustice, Joel. I apologize," he said, and went out of the room.

I left, too, and went into my room. I felt empty, sucked dry, and a depression came over me that I could not reason away. Captain Preftake was a good, decent man, yet his whole world had been toppled about him these last few minutes. Without raising his voice, without making a single threat, without deviating from the hurtful truth, Jim Wade had spoken words that would rankle and fester in Douglas Preftake's mind until he could no longer bear to think of them. Jim had seen that his own weak spot and Douglas Preftake's weak spot were the same: more than anything in the world they wanted Ellen to be happy. And Jim had used this knowledge cruelly, and to his own advantage; he had struck unerringly. I almost hated Jim Wade then, but beyond that I hated the necessity for these words having to be spoken.

Six

Mr. Tressel arrived at the garrison next morning. Within an hour after his arrival came news that the investigator for the leases had been appointed by President Cleveland. It was Lieutenant-General Philip Sheridan.

Mr. Tressel was unpacking his valise when Jim came back from the doorway where Mr. Edmonds' messenger had delivered the news. Mr. Tressel's old face was filled with a grim dismay as he heard Jim out, and the look he gave Jim held consternation. He abandoned his unpacking and we adjourned to the front porch of the post, on which were gathered most of the stockmen.

These were Texas men, and many of them had fought in the Civil War. Mr. Tressel had fought four long years, and all of Jim's kin had fought and some of them had died for the Confederacy. Lieutenant-General Sheridan had been a Union commander, but it was not that which disturbed these men. It was Sheridan's post-war career, when he was military commander of Louisiana and Texas during the reconstruction days, that they were remembering. Save General Sherman, whose excesses on his march to the sea might have been condoned as a military necessity, no man was as cordially hated by the South as Lieutenant-General Philip Sheridan, now the ranking army man of the country. His reconstruction administration had been so merciless that President Johnson could not stomach it, and had recalled him. This, then, was the man to whom Jim Wade was to look for justice. All that day and for many days after, these ranchers talked, and they looked to Jim for leadership. A petition of protest at the President's choice of an examiner was voted down, largely through Jim's influence, because he thought it would prejudice a successor against what was really our sound case.

In the long hot days following, I did not even have Lieutenant Tom Wynant's company as a relief from the interminable talk. He had been sent with the party that was surveying the Kiowa-Comanche-Cheyenne-Arapaho boundary. Jim was almost never alone. Every man who had leased land from the Indians – and there was a score of them – had come to the garrison. Hour after hour of interminable arguing took place. The Indian chiefs were sent for and sounded out, and slowly we prepared our case.

It was ready when Lieutenant-General Sheridan arrived a few days later. A relay of army ambulances brought him from the rail-head, and he was received at Reno with all the fanfare a remote garrison can provide for the highest-in-command. There was an inspection, of course, under the blazing summer sun where all the civilians were given the chance to see him. On horseback, his appearance was imposing, if deceptive. He had massive shoulders, a big head, and a high-colored face whose distinction was heightened by an imperial and a mustache. He sat his horse like the general he was, and his sharp brown eyes were as alert as the most anxious subaltern's. But afoot, his presence shrank, for he was a small man, under five and a half feet, and his size turned out to be, in part, girth of belly. He had a small man's aggressiveness of manner and movement even in this sultry heat, and when he took off his black army hat to mop a head of close-cropped iron-gray hair, there was something of the martinet in his appearance.

The investigation began immediately, and we waited uneasily through those hot summer days for some inkling of the findings. Everybody was questioned, and the army orderlies were constantly roving the hotel and post and the bars in search of witnesses. The nights were gay with festivities, which neither Jim nor Mr. Tressel nor I attended. I believe most of our nights during that time were spent in reviewing the witnesses and hazarding guesses as to the evidence for or against us that they had presented.

The Indian chiefs, big and little, friendly and hostile to us, were called, and of course the army contractors. Santee was quizzed long and hard, and when he was at last finished and had disappeared from the garrison, Jim was called.

He got up lazily from his chair on the porch when the orderly told him he was wanted, and walked with the soldier across the parade grounds, a tall, loose-built man carrying his hat in his hand. Nobody would have suspected from his appearance he was on his way to defend his million-dollar gamble, defend it with all the cunning and courage of which he was capable. That session of Jim's was not a short one. He went in at midmorning, and time was taken out for lunch, which he ate with Major Corning. Along toward late afternoon I was called.

The room where the investigation was being held was a moderately big one, and Sheridan lounged in his chair behind a table covered with papers. A man stenographer was taking down every word of the proceedings, and General Sheridan was flanked by army men of lesser rank.

I was seated next to Jim across the table from General Sheridan, and the questioning was resumed. I had been called to verify Jim's story of the killing of the chief's son and the ensuing grass fire. General Sheridan was a sharp questioner, although a polite one, and while his helpers seemed bored with my story and with the heat and the monotonous reiteration of events they had already heard explained, Sheridan listened carefully. As I talked I saw the perspiration bead his brown eyebrows, and several times he wiped his florid face with his big handkerchief, but he listened. When I had finished he thanked me courteously for coming, and as I went out I heard him direct an orderly to bring in one of the Cheyenne subchiefs, and then direct questions to Jim again.

That night Jim was calm. He told me that his questioners had been fair enough, but that he had had the impression all this day that he was talking to men whose minds were already made up. He went back the next morning, and at noon he finished by summing up our case, which was, in brief, this:

We alone were paying tens of thousands of dollars directly to the Indians for leases on grass which they could not possibly use. Far from fomenting trouble with the Indians, our influence was a peaceable one, for we were giving them beef and money that they had to have, and with which the government would not supply them. Our grass payments had been prompt, and we had been law abiding, save in those cases when self-defense was necessary. Our only defamers were the men who wanted what we had, and their former practice had been to pay the Indians in cheap whiskey instead of hard cash. The Indians were in favor of continuing the leases, except for the usual malcontents. If the Indians were restive, the fault did not lie with us, but with a government which would not keep its word to feed them. Jim said all this, and after that there was nothing to do but wait. And wait.

Those days were hell for Jim. Inaction for any length of time could set his eyes to simmering with unrest, so that I was surprised at the invariable gentleness of his answers to my questions. During those times he would have the appearance of a man ready to explode at the least provocation, and he would drink more than usual. But now he did not drink, nor did he talk. Preftake's house was visible across the parade ground from the front porch of the store, and hour after hour Jim would sit out there watching it. So far as I knew he had not seen Ellen since we came back to Reno, although I learned later that he and Ellen had talked for twenty minutes on the porch of the trading post in front of anyone who cared to watch them.

But I did not know of that meeting then, and I wondered why, if he loved Ellen, he did not go to her now, when she needed him. It never occurred to me during those long, oven-hot days that the very words Jim had spoken to Captain Preftake that night also kept him from seeing Ellen. He had said that he would wait, that sooner or later Douglas Preftake, seeing Ellen's unhappiness, would give her the freedom she wanted. By staying away from Ellen, Jim was compounding her unhappiness for Doug to see.

And then the thing happened that was to give Jim a drive and a direction and change his life and all our lives.

It was only days after Sheridan left, with no published conclusions as to his investigation, that the bombshell exploded.

The news came over the army telegraph and Major Corning himself brought it to us in the hotel restaurant where most of the stockmen, weary with the mid-July heat and impatient for news, were gathered.

Major Corning, from beside our table, announced to the whole room that President Cleveland had issued a proclamation that all leases on the Cheyenne-Arapaho reservation were void, and that the leases must be vacated in forty days.

It almost brought a riot from these men whose nerves were already wire-edged. Chairs were overturned and a tumult of shouting filled the room as the men flocked to our table.

Stunned, I looked at Jim, who was regarding Major Corning with an expression of utter disbelief. Then he spoke, and his voice overrode the angry babbling of the others and silenced them, and it was not the voice of anger so much as the voice of a man cajoling a dangerous idiot.

"But Major, he can't do that!"

"The telegrapher got a repeat, Jim. I'm afraid he has."

Then the angry storm broke.

"Does Mr. Cleveland know that every acre of graze in the Cherokee Outlet and lower Kansas is already leased?"

"Where will we move?"

"It takes a whole summer for a steer to locate himself on new range. If he doesn't know his shelter, he'll die in dirty weather."

"We can't move in that time!"

"It'll ruin us!"

Jim slapped his hand on the table so violently the silver jumped. "I've got sixty thousand head of steers up from Texas. Where will I move them?" he demanded savagely.

Major Corning raised his hand. "Gentlemen, gentlemen. I'm only a Major. I couldn't change the President's orders if I wanted to."

Jim wasn't listening. He stood up now, and all the color was gone from his lips and face. "I don't believe it," he said flatly.

"I'm afraid it's true," Major Corning spoke patiently, sympathetically.

Jim looked at him blankly. All the other ranchers were watching Jim, just as I was.

"But Major," Jim said gently. "If we have to get out, we'll get out. But give us time. Time!" He put both hands on the table and leaned toward the Major, desperation in his face. "Man, can't you understand! We can't take our cattle back to Texas, for nobody will buy them back on this market. We can't take them north, for there is no place to take them. All the grass is taken. We can't ship them, for nobody will buy them, trail gaunted like they are. And we've got to do one of these in forty days!"

He slowly came erect, and shook his head briefly. "I don't believe it. I don't believe it a man as big as President Cleveland would do that, knowing what it will mean to us."

Major Corning stood up. "I'm sorry, Jim. But my orders are to enforce the evacuation at the end of the forty-day period, with soldiers if necessary."

In utter silence, Major Corning departed.

Jim stood there, his eyes hotly musing, and the other ranchers could only look at each other in mute incomprehension. For them, the smaller of them, the decree meant terrible hardships. But for us, with sixty thousand head of trail cattle to move, with no place to move them, and with no time to locate them, it was catastrophe. Jim Wade's great dream had unfolded into a nightmare.

Jim said suddenly in a firm voice, "I don't believe any man would do that knowingly – not any man."

"Then somebody ought to tell him," Mr. Tressel said sharply.

"Somebody is," Jim answered. "I am. I'm going to Washington." He looked over the group of cattlemen. "He'll listen to a delegation from us ranchers. He's got to."

"I'll go, too," one of the ranchers said. Three others, whose interests were fairly large, volunteered also.

Then the reaction set in, and these men began to curse the President, Sheridan, and the army. But that was not Jim's way. His first move was to telegraph the Senator to get the machinery of protest in motion. He telegraphed Mr. Satterfield, too. While the others left the restaurant for the bar, their bitterness and outrage hourly more vocal, Jim began quietly to fight. He wasn't down yet. He had bet everything he had and could get on an unsure thing, counting on his luck and brains. But now, when it looked as if he had bet wrong, he was not conceding defeat. All that long afternoon in his room, while I dared not think what this meant to the company, Jim laid his plans. He gave us minute directions to follow in his absence. Try as I might, I could not tell if he believed that his trip to Washington would win us temporary pardon or not. But he was fighting, not whining.

Toward evening, Jim and I made ready to leave for Caldwell. It was the custom here during the summer to travel at night, when the heat had lessened, and we planned to leave after supper.

Immediately after we had eaten in company with the other four ranchers who made up the delegation, Jim rose and told us to saddle up, that he would be with us shortly.

I followed him as far as the porch. I saw him in the late dusk cross the parade ground, and he was heading straight for the Preftakes. By the time he returned to the wagon yard, our horses were saddled. His face betrayed nothing to me, but I knew he had seen Ellen, and I wondered how.

Not once on that long ride to Caldwell did he betray any optimism over the trip to Washington, or any pessimism either. Where the others

161

of our party, by mutual condolences and assurances, managed to jack up their spirits and mine, Jim was silent. My mind was filled with it, and by slow degrees I began to believe that the President would grant us the pardon we needed – a winter to graze our beef on the range they were used to before we moved out in the spring.

At Caldwell, Jim arranged for them to ride East on a cattle train that was just making up, and I said goodbye to him as we stood on the cinder right of way by the caboose in the blazing sun of afternoon, the rails radiating an acrid, iron-smelling heat. We shook hands and I wished him luck, and I think my voice was a little excited with the importance of his errand and the prospects of my own job here.

About to swing up on the platform, he paused and said gravely, "Joey, drop in on Ellen when you're in Reno next, will you?"

Those were his last words before the train pulled out.

Seven

The job Mr. Tressel and I were left to do was a big one. There were fifty thousand head of single- and double-wintered beeves that must be shipped immediately, regardless of a market that probably would never rise again. To do it, Mr. Tressel had to have ten round-up crews, which I must hire in Caldwell and Dodge City, outfit and send down to him on the lease.

By the time I had done this, the first of our many trail herds was arriving in Caldwell. Shipping these herds as they arrived, keeping books for twelve outfits, and outfitting – all in the hot, long days of a dusty summer – filled my time.

It was during a lull, when the herds on the northwest corner of our lease were being driven to Dodge City for shipment, that I seized the opportunity to go to Reno to straighten out some credit matters with Edmonds Brothers. Before I left Caldwell I went to the post office, as I had done every day since Jim left, on hopes there would be some news from him regarding our lease. There was a letter from him, and it was brief, saying only that they had an audience with President Cleveland arranged for two days hence, and that their reception at both the War and Interior departments had been sympathetic. There was also a letter from Elizabeth Lowell, which informed me she would return from Boston in the fall. It said precious little else, and I could tell from its restraint that while I had not exactly offended her by not writing, I had come close enough to make it uncomfortable for us both.

I did not realize until I took the stage and sat back on the seat to relax just how hard I had been working. The heat of the summer had been savage, and I had gone sleepless too many nights and foodless too many days for it not to tell on me. I was so tired I contrived to sleep on the stage, a feat in itself.

Arriving at Reno, I found that things had been happening in my absence. Mr. Coe had been dismissed as agent – another result of Sheridan's investigation – and the agent's post filled by an army man, Captain Ford. With new troops to back him Ford had put an end to the Indian threat.

I straightened out matters with Mr. Edmonds the first evening. Next day, finding that Lieutenant Tom Wynant was still on the survey of the boundary between the Cheyenne-Arapaho,

Kiowa-Comanche reservation, I paid my respects to Captain Ford at Darlington.

With all my business and social calls off my hands, I turned to what was the real reason for my coming. I was going to see Ellen, and it was not wholly because Jim had asked me to. I had missed her, and in a different way I think I hungered for her as much as Jim did. This presented a problem, for I was Jim Wade's friend and employee, and Ellen was still Captain Preftake's wife. But a summer of responsibility had developed a need and a liking for bluntness in me, so I went to Captain Preftake at his office.

He was surprised to see me, and I think pleased, and I had long since forgotten our animosity in Caldwell and here. He had the same slow likable way of talking, the same direct way of looking at me, but there was a kind of haunting soberness of expression in his face that he couldn't have hidden from anyone.

"Captain Preftake," I began, after the amenities were concluded, "I've come to ask a favor of you."

"What's that, Joel?"

"I wanted your permission to see Ellen." Maybe it was a clumsy way of putting it, but as I have said, I had come to like bluntness.

"By all means. You have it." He paused, and added with a kind of shy gruffness, "You needn't have asked, Joey."

"I didn't want to – well" – I found myself suddenly confused – "I have always liked Ellen, and she and you have both been kind to me. I didn't want you to think that I was acting as a messenger – or – or was presuming on my acquaintance."

It was clumsy at best, but he understood. He said quietly and frankly, "I'll always be ashamed of that, Joel. I haven't apologized enough to you for what happened, and it doesn't seem as if I can."

"It was natural."

"But not excusable." He smiled wryly, and then said something that made me sure I had never been wrong in liking him. "It's hard to always see where the right lies, Joey. I'm still trying."

I rose then, and he invited me to dinner that night. I told him I was leaving on the midafternoon stage, and that this was the reason for my request, and I thanked him. We parted friends, and we stayed friends, strangely enough.

I went over to the Preftakes' square stone house, and I was admitted by a colored servant. When Ellen came into the room, there was a delight in her face that made her radiant. She kissed me, embarrassing me, and then, as she had done before, drew off to look at me. Only I was in the role of examiner this time, and I did not like what I saw. She was thinner, more beautiful too, if that was possible, but she was not happy. The very spontaneity and joy of her welcome told me that she had been starved for friendship, for sympathy, for something to release and lift her spirit. I was bound that I would do just that, if possible, and my first thought was to get her away from the garrison.

So I said, presently, that I had come to take her for a drive. She was delighted, and pleaded time to change her clothes. I left for the stables to hire a top buggy, and when I returned with one she was waiting for me. We drove down toward Darlington, but at the bottomlands of the Canadian we took the road following the river to the wood reserve, and were soon in the drowsy shade of the big cottonwoods. Where the road swung in toward one of the low bluffs that overlooked the long sweep of the sandy river bed we pulled aside and got out and found a place where we could sit. Ellen was wearing a white cotton dress with blue flower sprays, and I offered my coat, which I was glad to take off in the heat, for her to sit on.

"My second buggy ride with you, Joel. Do you remember the first one?" she asked.

"I do. We came along this same road."

"You were a very opinionated young man that night. About the life at army posts, your girl and Jim."

This was the first mention of Jim, and when she mentioned his name she looked at me, and I could see a wild hunger in her eyes.

I looked away and she went on in a voice subtly changed, as if she were making a desperate effort to keep it light and casual. "You didn't like the country, I remember, and you were boosting for railroads and . . . and . . ." Her voice broke and I looked up quickly.

"Joey, what's going to happen to me?" she cried. It was the cry of someone lost — heartbroken and sad and lost.

It was terrifying to hear her, and I knew the old Ellen was gone, that the spirit of her was starving. Nothing could nourish it except Jim, except being with him always.

"You could wait once," I said. "It won't be so long."

"Long? It'll be until Doug dies!"

She beat the ground with her small fist and she did not know she was doing it. She was looking at me as if pleading for help, but I could give her none and she knew it.

She looked away from me toward the river and the far bluff, and began to talk in a tight, strange voice.

"The night Jim left he came over to see me, Joey. Doug was there. He asked Doug again to divorce me, and asked him for both of us. And Doug refused. Twice since then I've asked him, and both times he's refused. He won't even talk about it now."

"He hates giving you up?"

"That and divorce itself."

I had hated the thought of it too, ever since Jim had mentioned it. And now, knowing only that I had to say it, I blurted out, "It is ugly, Ellen. It's dirty."

She turned her face to me and said with a curious, cold intensity, "What's clean about the way I'm living now?"

I couldn't answer that, but I persisted. "It would follow you, Ellen. Have you thought of that? That no matter where Jim took you, people would know. Good women don't divorce their husbands."

"I'm not a good woman," Ellen said quietly.

"You're the best I know."

"No." She shook her head vehemently. "If I were a good woman, I would be with Jim now, instead of waiting for Doug to change his mind."

She leaned forward now, and talked with a passionate conviction. "Do you think I don't know what's happening to Jim? He's fighting for his very life, for the thing he's staked years and his sweat and brains to build. I watched them crucify him at the investigation. I know what's happening now. I know too that he'll never need me as much as he does now. And I wait — and don't help him!"

She was crying now, trying to hold it back. She said in a quavering, bitter voice, "I'm no good to him, Joey! I'm no good!"

Then it came, and she put her face in her hands and cried. I knelt by her and tried to comfort her, but I could not stop her sobbing. She didn't need me or my comfort; she needed Jim.

I left her and walked over to the bluff, kicking savagely at anything in my way. Perhaps I should have been more philosophical, for there was no way out of it for them. But I was young, and I could only be viciously angry at something I could not name, and wild with a desire to fight it.

When I came back to Ellen she had stopped crying, and there was only a terrible sadness in her face.

She put out a hand to me and said, "Pull me up, Joey. We've got to go."

"Ellen," I said when she faced me, "make Jim take you out of here! Make him take you to Texas, Doug or no Doug!"

She looked at me a brief moment, and then put her arms around me and hugged me tightly, desperately. Then she turned and walked toward the buggy. It was over and I knew that my last words had been foolish. Jim wouldn't take her while she was Doug's wife, although she would have been willing to go, and nothing she could say would make him change his mind. It came to me then that I had made the full circle again; I was begging her to make Jim take her away, when only months ago it was the thing I feared most. I could not even trust myself.

Afterwards we drove on along the river for a ways, but it was no use pretending we enjoyed the ride. I turned around soon and we drove back to the garrison, wordless in a communion of unhappiness. I remembered one other occasion when our ride had ended like this, Ellen remembered it too.

At her door she said goodbye and she watched me drive off. I don't know which of us felt and looked the more forlorn.

Rounding the corner of the parade grounds, I had an overwhelming desire to get out of here, and quickly. It was unreasoning and childish and I knew I had no reason to run away, but this place would always seem a prison to me and Ellen Preftake the prisoner.

Passing the long porch before the sutler's bar, I eyed the usual row of loafers in their back-tilted chairs with distaste. I recognized Santee Paddock in the line; he was talking earnestly to the man beside him, gesturing with his cigar. If he saw me, he gave no sign of recognition.

I paid for my livery rental and went into the

hotel. The clerk at the desk informed me a Mr. Cantrell had called three times during the morning, inquiring after me. Since I did not know the name, it did not impress me.

I ate and then returned to my room to pack my few belongings and pass the hour or so until stage time. Already my imagination was leaping ahead to the time when Jim would learn of Ellen's despair today, and I wondered if that was what he wanted.

I had finished my meager packing and was sitting despondently on the edge of the bed when a knock sounded on my room door. I did not know the man who presented himself, although there was something vaguely familiar about him. He was agreeable and polite enough in his greeting.

"Mr. Hardy? I'm Mr. Cantrell."

My face evidently showed that his name was not familiar to me and he added, "I'm the representative of Shore Brothers in Arkansas City."

We had done business with them during the fencing of the lease and since, I remembered, and I shook hands with him and invited him into the room. He was dressed in a black suit and he looked uncomfortably hot, but I did not ask him to sit down, and I hoped his business would be short.

He took a chair nevertheless, and inquired

172

after the affairs of the company, and I answered as noncommittally as I could. Presently, after further talk on the heat and the lack of summer rains, he came down to business.

"I saw your name on the register, Mr. Hardy, and thought we might clean up a little business. I have here" — he reached in his coat and brought out a paper to hand to me — "your account with us. Only seven hundred and some dollars, I believe. I thought I might take your check back with me."

I looked at the bill, which was for some wire for some drift fence, some feed, harness and tools. I said, "All right. I'll send you a check when I get back to Caldwell."

"I — I wonder if you'd mind much letting me have your check now, Mr. Hardy? Fact is, we're pressed for ready cash," he added diffidently and hurriedly, as he caught the surprise in my glance. "Things have been tight with us. We overstocked on the expectancy of a successful Boomer push into the Nations, and now we're being crowded ourselves."

I said with some irony: "We've been a pretty good customer of your firm, Mr. Cantrell. I can't really see that five days' lapse in time will make much difference."

"Exactly, Mr. Hardy," he said smoothly, purposely misunderstanding me. "It wouldn't make a bit of difference to you, and it will to us. I knew you'd look at it that way, if you knew we had pressing engagements to meet."

"I didn't mean that," I retorted in some confusion. When he looked surprised, and not a bit embarrassed my confusion increased, although I was aware his surprise was only expert acting. I blurted out, "I have no checkbook with me, Mr. Cantrell."

Before I finished saying it, he had a checkbook in hand, and it was of the Arkansas City bank with which we did business.

I was uncomfortably trapped, and I was considering further protest when I remembered that doubtless their bill was waiting at the office in Caldwell, and that I would pay it the day I returned anyway.

I took his checkbook and had written the date when it occurred to me that this was the second large check I had written in Reno within two days, the first to Mr. Edmonds. The presentation of the Edmonds' bill was not extraordinary; we made it a habit to deposit large amounts of money with him and draw on it through the store, its freighters, its feed business and such. Sometimes, as in this case, we had a large overdraft that had not entirely agreed with our books. It was not strange that Mr. Edmonds should want it straightened out, but why was Mr. Cantrell in such a hurry for his money? Did they believe the Canadian

Cattle Company wasn't solvent?

Pen poised over the checkbook, I felt an uneasiness that was close to alarm. I had always believed that Jim would get the time extension from Washington. Didn't they?

I resolved to bring things into the clear, and when I had written the check and handed it to him I said casually, "You'll be getting a sizable order from us soon, Mister Cantrell."

"On our new terms?" he murmured.

"And what are they?"

He avoided looking at me, but made an eloquent gesture of hands outspread, shoulders shrugged, and said, "Our creditors have got us over a barrel, Mr. Hardy. Our new terms, of necessity, are cash."

If I had had any suspicions, they were confirmed now. The Canadian Cattle Company in the eyes of the Shore Brothers was a poor credit risk.

When Cantrell had gone, I sat on the edge of the bed for many minutes, wondering why his face was so familiar. At last it came to me. When I had left Ellen and driven to the livery stable and seen Santee on the porch, this Mr. Cantrell was the man with whom he was talking. At the thought that Santee might be behind Mr. Cantrell's call, my mind was angrily made up.

Putting on my coat, I went down to the

officer's bar. Mr. Cantrell was in lackadaisical conversation with an army man as I came in, and he nodded to me.

I went on through the saloon, and by the time I had reached the porch I was somehow certain that Santee Paddock had got Mr. Cantrell's ear. Looking along the porch past the usual line of early afternoon loafers I saw that Santee was still in his chair, staring moodily across the parade grounds. I went over and took a chair beside him, and he greeted me curtly, indifferently.

I didn't speak for a moment, not trusting my temper. But the longer I waited, the angrier I got, and besides, no clever way of approaching the subject occurred to me. I plunged into it then, not caring how transparent my motives were.

"Wasn't that Mr. Cantrell of Arkansas City who was sitting with you when I passed in the buggy, Mr. Paddock?" I asked.

"Why, he's been talking with me, yes. Left a few minutes ago." He turned his head to observe me with those hooded, wary eyes of his.

"Business isn't so good with his house, I hear."

"It's exceptionally fine," Santee said in blunt contradiction.

"Either he's a liar, then, or it's improved within the last ten minutes," I said with some asperity.

"He's dunned you and refused your further credit, I take it," Santee murmured drily.

"He has," I said bluntly. "How did you know?"

"I told him to collect while he could."

He surveyed me with perfectly frank dislike. Curiously, I was not surprised at his confession, and in a way I was glad of it, because it gave me a chance to say some things that perhaps I would not have said otherwise.

"Mr. Paddock," I began, "you've put the Indians against us, and all the white people around here. You've tried to ruin us, and haven't even balked at murder for a weapon. You've tried to ruin Jim Wade, and I doubt if you'll succeed. You —"

"Don't be too sure I won't," Santee said calmly.

"Don't be too sure you will," I replied, just as calmly. "You won't be the first renegade white Jim Wade has helped hang."

Santee's hands gripped the arms of his chair and he started out of his seat. I came up quickly, but he did not get up. He had control of himself again when I faced him, but the telltale banners of red in his cheekbones told me I had scored.

"You young pup," he said quietly, through closed teeth. "Get out of here before I lose my temper."

"Having lost all honor, that's all you have left to lose," I said. Whereupon, I turned and left him and went up to my room. My satisfaction in winning this name-calling contest lasted until I reached the top of the stairs, but by the time I reached my room I was thinking of its graver side. Santee now dared to openly insult us, even taking our downfall for granted. Merchants were risking offending us by closing our credit and dunning us. All this in the face of the fact that when Jim got our time extension we would be on the lease through the winter and into the spring. I had believed with absolute faith that President Cleveland, when he learned the facts, would extend the time limit of the evacuation order. Now, in the privacy of my room, I experienced my first doubts. Did Santee have information denied me? Mr. Cantrell's action argued so. I remembered Santee's words: "I told him to collect while he could." If Cantrell was on the right trail, then it wouldn't take the banks long to follow suit. Fighting down my growing panic, I had the sense to see what I should do. I must find Mr. Tressel immediately and lay the facts before him.

Eight

Three days later I rode into our roundup camp on a rented horse. As I neared the wagon I saw Mr. Tressel in conversation with one of the new trail bosses I had hired. He did not see me, and as I dismounted I was shocked to see the change in him. He was unshaven, wearing the same faded denim of his meanest rider. He was gaunter, and seemed more frail even then usual, and I suddenly realized that the burden of shipping these sixty thousand head had fallen mainly on him. If Jim had doubled and tripled my work, it was only to ease Mr. Tressel's almost intolerable burden

The trail boss saw me first, and smiled and said, "Howdy, Mr. Hardy."

When Mr. Tressel caught sight of me his eyes lighted up and he shook hands warmly with me. He finished giving orders to the foreman, and we retired to seats on the tongue of the roundup wagon. I plunged into my story immediately, and Mr. Tressel heard me out in silence. His tired old face was so expressionless that I ended up by saying lamely, "Maybe I shouldn't have come, Mr. Tressel. Only I wanted you to know."

"What was it again that Santee said?"

I told him, and he stroked the white beard-stubble of his chin. "I know this Cantrell. I know the Shores too. They wouldn't risk offending us on a rumor."

"If we don't know what's happened at Washington, how can Santee?" I asked.

"I think there'll be news from Jim in Caldwell," Mr. Tressel said.

"You think I should go back right away?"

"We'll both go," he said, rising. He smiled wryly. "If it's true that things have gone against us in Washington, Joey, then the wolves will start howling." He added grimly, but not without kindliness, "I know how to fight 'em off a little better than you."

We started for Caldwell as soon as Mr. Tressel had given the foreman his orders. There were enough shipping beeves in this area to make up two more herds, and Mr. Tressel could leave safely.

It began to rain in the night of our first day out, and the rest of the ride in the slow, drought-breaking drizzle was pure misery. We were nearly waterbound at the Salt Fork of the Arkansas, but we got across. A half-day later and we could not have done so. This was my first taste of a plainsman's life when all was not perfect. Wet clothes, wet saddle, wet blankets, mud, dripping shelter, insufficient fire and the meager rations of a hurried journey I could tolerate, but the low blanket of sky, the rain-laden grass and the solitude sank my spirits. It seemed as if we had been turned loose on the day of Creation. Man had not left his mark here yet, and it was too big.

It was still raining the night we rode into the mire of Caldwell's streets where the light from the store lamps was reflected in the restless pools of water, and the movement of the town was all between the wooden awnings of the stores.

Putting up our horses we slogged wearily over to the Drover's House, and left a trail of mud and water across the warm lobby on the way to the desk.

The clerk saw us and smiled and said, "Mr. Wade is in room eight, Mr. Tressel," as if he supposed we knew of Jim's arrival.

We forgot all else in our haste to see Jim. Upstairs, the knock on his door was answered by his voice and we stepped into a large room that held, besides Jim slouched in an easy chair, four other men.

I got only the briefest glimpse of Jim's face before it lighted up at sight of us, and it was tired and somber. He came over to us and gripped Mr. Tressel's hand and squeezed my arm at the same time, and then he turned to the men.

"We'd better adjourn this until tomorrow morning, gentlemen."

I knew some of these men and all of them had one thing in common. They were the type peculiar to frontier towns, the solid merchants and professional men who backed their more adventurous brethren with money and goods, and usually came out of it rich. They had another thing in common this night; they did not want to leave, and they were in uniformly bad humor. Jim stood there, adamant, until the leader picked up his coat and hat off the dresser and filed past us with a curt nod of recognition to Mr. Tressel.

When Jim closed the door behind them, Mr. Tressel said quietly, "No luck, Jim?"

"No luck," Jim echoed.

"You mean we don't get the extension?" I asked.

"Forty days from last July twentieth, we've got to be off the lease," Jim said. He only glanced briefly, almost apologetically, at Mr. Tressel, and then crossed the room to the chair again. Mr. Tressel, in silence, took off his coat, while I stood there not knowing what to say. Not for one moment since I had heard Jim say in the dining room of the hotel in Reno, "He can't do that," had I believed this would come to pass. I had feared it a little in these last few days, but I did not believe it.

"What happened, Jim?" Mr. Tressel said, after he had sat on the bed facing Jim.

Briefly, his voice flat with weariness Jim told what took place in Washington. The delegation, with the aid of our Senator, had been granted an interview with President Cleveland. Jim laid before the President the simple facts, that all the stockmen were willing to vacate the lease, but to vacate it within the time limit set would mean ruin for them all. President Cleveland asked him the reason for this, and Jim explained that "locating" southern cattle anew at this late date was tantamount to losing them, even if range could be found, which was not likely. By extending the time limit and allowing them to winter on the lease where they were "locating," the stockmen would pass a safe winter and sell and ship in the spring.

President Cleveland was sympathetic, but was firm in his desire that no backward step should be taken in settling the problem. Argument and persuasion followed, and finally the President excused himself to consult with his staff. He returned in an hour, and gave his final, stubborn word. If he had known the hardships entailed to stockmen when he gave the order, he would never have signed the evacuation order; but now that it was signed, he must stand by it. No pleading could change him, and angry words passed, one of the delegation refusing to shake hands with the President as he left.

When Jim finished, Mr. Tressel said nothing. He was thinking, we were all of us thinking, that the half million dollars in beef that we had on the lease was as good as lost. We had received justice, not mercy.

Jim rose and went to the window, looking out onto the rainy night. Mr. Tressel murmured wrathfully, "I never thought I'd want to shoot a President."

I never heard Jim, then or later, second Mr. Tressel's sentiments, although he had every right to hold himself the victim of stupidity and stubborn prejudice. That great cattle empire, which he had built with work and humor and skepticism, too, had vanished; and now he was just another man, tired with too much defeat, facing an impossible situation.

He had his back to me, looking out the window into the night, and I was almost afraid to have him turn around. I had seen Jim's face in times of trouble; I did not want to see it in this time of disaster. But when he turned his head to look at Mr. Tressel, I saw he was frowning, his gray eyes alert in scheming.

"Harry, how far can you carry blackmail?" he asked.

Mr. Tressel didn't understand, and neither did I.

"There's range out there," Jim murmured, nodding his head toward the window. "That bunch of buzzards that begged for stock in our company are goin' to get it for me, too, or else I'll dump sixty thousand head of cattle in their laps and quit."

Mr. Tressel considered this a long moment. "They might be able to. Last winter was an uncertain one. The market's been bad and nobody's stocked up much this summer." He looked glumly at Jim. "Suppose you do. We still have to face the chance of a hard winter."

Jim laughed shortly, humorlessly. "Hell, it couldn't be harder than the government's heart."

It was the same tough, indomitable Jim Wade who took an hour of that night telling us we weren't at the end of our rope yet. Our local stockholders, he pointed out, were at our mercy, for their assets were tied up in sixty thousand head of beef that they were no more able to take care of than we were. Their only hope of breaking even on their investment was to see that these cattle were wintered safely. The stockholders must be assessed and the creditors put to work getting us range in the Cherokee Outlet (not included in the evacua-

185

tion order), buying, leasing or bribing grass for our cattle. After that, we must all trust to a mild winter to pull us through.

And that was the plan Jim hammered on through the following days when our creditors met. Many of these men, I learned from Mr. Tressel, had begged Jim to allow them to buy stock in the Canadian Cattle Company beyond the sums they had loaned Jim when he expanded. Jim had done so as a favor, and his brains and success had carried some of them to fortunes. But that was forgotten now.

All the days I spent at the office doing book work, Jim and Mr. Tressel shuttled between smoke-filled hotel rooms and the station telegraph office. I saw little of them, except to learn that they were gradually winning the stockholders and creditors over to our side.

And then late one afternoon, Jim came up to the office, smelling of whiskey and cigars, and I was sitting in the big chair. As in the past, I had worked myself out of something to do and was again at the law books, this time more listlessly than before.

Jim saw the book and grinned, and it was almost like old times when he drawled. "There ain't a prison term for what we're doin', Joey, so you don't need to look it up."

I laughed and said, "Just what are we doing?"

"Tomorrow, you and me are startin' for the

lease." For a moment that old impudence lighted his gray eyes. "You and me are going to lead sixty thousand Israelite beeves out of the Promised Land."

That was the last of the old care-free Jim Wade that I was to see.

Mr. Tressel remained in Caldwell to take over my job, while we left to start the big clean-up of the lease. When the remaining single- and double-wintered beeves were shipped, there were three million acres to comb for sixty thousand cattle to move a hundred miles north into the Cherokee Outlet. We couldn't hope to meet the deadline; and part of the reason for Jim's going was to plead for an extension of time.

During that long ride over the sear plains, we talked of everything except Ellen. We passed one of our trail herds on the way. Pete-Keach McCune bossing it, and he pessimistically confirmed Jim's view that we couldn't clean out the shipping stuff, let alone the "through" stuff before the deadline.

We pushed on to headquarters ranch and found it deserted except for Isom, who came out on crutches to meet us. His horse had thrown him in a stampede during a storm, and he was recuperating from a broken leg. As soon as he could hobble around, McCune had deserted him.

That night Isom told us of the rumors coming from Fort Reno. It was said that if we weren't moved off the lease by the deadline, Negro troops would be called to eject us and our cattle forcibly. Negro troops still made Texans see red, and Isom predicted that undeclared war was imminent, since, short-handed as we were in facing this heroic job, we couldn't hope to make the deadline.

Jim listened grimly and said nothing, but next morning he told us to saddle up to go to Reno with him. He was going to see Major Corning about extending the deadline, and to hire as many men as he could as earnest of his intentions to clear the lease in compliance with the law.

We dragged into Reno on the tail end of a smoking hot day, and after supper Jim disappeared. I turned in, dead tired, but the oven-hot room, still holding the heat of the day, would not let me sleep. After an hour of wakefulness, during which I did nothing but imagine Jim's meeting with Ellen — for I was certain he was seeing her — I got up and dressed and, drugged by the heat, stumbled downstairs.

With a whole evening to pass I hunted up Lieutenant Tom Wynant, who had not heard of our coming. He was tanned and rugged looking from his stretch on boundary duty, and we adjourned to the sutler's bar, the coolest place in the post.

It was a long narrow room, with card tables against the big, many-paned windows that would have looked out onto the porch save that their lower halves were painted opaque. The bar was against the opposite wall, and was backed by a handsome stretch of mirror. Professional gamblers had been driven out of the garrison, but there were still games to be had and they were being played tonight by a scattering of army officers and agency men.

Tom and I ordered our beers and took a vacant table, relaxed, and yarned about our adventures. I talked too much, because I was trying not to think of Ellen and Jim.

Midway in the evening, Santee Paddock, in company with three other men, tramped into the barroom and took places at the end of the bar nearest the door. The room was filling up, and presently the bartender came over and asked if we would mind giving up our table to some men who wanted to play cards, and wait for a smaller table to be vacated.

Tom grinned, and, knowing the etiquette of such occasions, said, "If they're friends of ours, Charlie, we'd be glad to. Who wants to play?"

"Mr. Paddock and some friends, sir."

A subtle change came over Tom's face. He said, "Yes, we would mind giving it up, Charlie."

I thought I saw a trace of a pleased smile in the bartender's broad face as he said, "Yes, sir," and went back to the bar.

"You don't like Mr. Paddock, then, Tom?"

He shook his head. "I do not. And not only because of Jim. He's getting to be a man of too much substance, Joey. He doesn't wear it well, and I'm not the only man who thinks so."

I saw the bartender speak to Santee, who turned to look at us, spoke to one of his companions, and then took the ten steps to confront us at our table.

"Evening," he said to us both, first removing his unlighted cigar from his mouth.

We both spoke civilly.

"We'd like a game of cards, gentlemen. Maybe you'd like to join us," Santee said.

"No, thanks," I said.

"No, thanks," Tom said.

Santee, bland as always said, "Then maybe you'd do us the courtesy of giving up your table."

Tom stared up at Santee and said, "Mr. Paddock, this bar was put in here for the pleasure of the garrison officers. I happen to be a garrison officer and it's my pleasure to sit at this table."

The roomful of men, who were aware that something out of the ordinary was taking place, quieted. Santee, however, ignored it, and inclined his head in recognition of Tom's answer.

"Your name is Lieutenant Wynant, isn't it?"

Tom nodded.

"Well, Lieutenant Wynant, I don't usually discuss my business with outsiders, but I purchased this bar concession from Mr. Edmonds last week." His voice took on a sudden edge as he spoke into the silence. "I have never liked the idea of small-beer customers taking up the playing tables. Shall we begin changing that right now?"

Leisurely, Tom rose, saying, "So you own this bar now?"

"I do."

"It's a pity that I'm going to have to give up drinking while I'm so young, then," Tom drawled.

The laughter wasn't loud, but there was enough of it and it was genuine enough to bring the color into Santee's thick neck. I rose, to leave with Tom.

"No need to do that, Lieutenant," Santee said in a bland, arrogant voice. "Just pay a little less attention to your friend's roostering." He turned his big head to look at me, his hooded eyes baleful.

My face went hot and I tried to keep my voice normal as I said, "Any roostering I do, Santee, will be in public and not behind your back."

"But from behind Jim Wade's back, eh?" Santee said drily. The room was dead quiet now; even the bartender had ceased his clatter.

"He's not here now," I pointed out in a tight voice.

"That's right, he isn't," Santee drawled. "Where is he? With his woman?"

"I'm right here, Santee."

Every man in that room, including Santee, looked toward the doorway. Jim was lounging against the jamb of the door that opened into the store at the side of the bar. I do not know how long he had been there.

Santee moved to the corner of the bar and stopped there, his three friends beside him. Jim straightened up at his approach, and for all the faint smile on his pale face, there was murder in his eyes.

"I interrupted you," Jim drawled. "What were you saying?"

I wanted to shout, "Don't, Jim!" because I knew if Santee elaborated, then Jim and Ellen's secret would be laid bare.

Santee considered this challenge for three long seconds, while his deep and lasting hatred for Jim crowded him into speech.

"I said I wondered if —"

That was all he got out. Jim lunged for him. Santee took a step backwards, his hand streaking for the gun in his belt. I yelled. But

Charlie, the bartender, acted.

With a length of sawed-off pool cue which he brought up from behind the bar, he leaned over and slashed down with it across Santee's body. It caught Santee's gun coming out of his trousers and swinging up in the arc that would end with a shot. At the impact the gun went off, pointed at the floor, and then ripped out of Santee's hand and skidded across the floor. And then Jim hit him a blow in the face that sent Santee off balance. He took two steps backward, lost his balance entirely, fell into our table and took it down with him.

Tom Wynant yelled, "Leave those guns alone, you!" and I saw that his service pistol was unlimbered and pointed at Santee's three friends, who backed off, their hands raising.

Jim didn't see Tom, didn't hear him. He was across the room as Santee, blood streaming out of his mashed nose, came up off the floor. Jim hit him again, this time knocking him over the table and into a chair where he was brought up sharply against the wall. And then Santee came up, his face twisted with fury, to meet Jim's rush.

His foot braced against the wall for leverage, Santee swung with all the power of his great hulking body, and Jim, his feet tangled in one of the chair rungs, went over backwards and fell sprawling.

Santee leaped for him and Jim rolled away and came to his feet, and then they were both face to face, toe to toe, slugging at each other in a wild abandon.

The only sounds were their great gusty grunts, the solid sickening smack of bone on flesh, the scraping of their feet on the floor. It was as if neither of them could feel the pain, or were both willing to bear it if they could give some in return. Santee, under the great sledging fists that Jim caromed off his face, was the first to give away. He backed up a little, and raised his forearm to protect his face. And Jim, with the patient skill of a butcher, drove a blow deep into Santee's midriff.

The sound of the breath driven out of Santee could be heard all over the room, and his gagging moan as he tried to get breath. His arms came away from his face in his effort and then Jim laced a looping blow at his face that drove him into the overturned table again. Santee tried to come erect, but Jim did not give him time. And the blow that Jim swung then had every ounce of his great strength behind it.

It caught Santee on the point of the jaw, and there was a thick awful sound of a muffled ripping. Santee screamed, but no noise came. That blow drove him through the great window, the sill catching him behind the knees; and he fell backwards through the window onto the porch in a jangle of showering glass.

Jim lunged through the window after him. I saw him pick Santee up, stand him up with a mighty heave at his coat and then hit him again. Santee went backwards off the porch.

I was the first man to head for the porch, and when I got there Jim was on the ground astride Santee, slugging his sodden face in exhausted and rhythmic fury.

Two other men and myself succeeded in dragging Jim off before he killed him, although then I was sure we were too late. Leaning on us, Jim stood weaving about Santee, his shirt torn off his back, his lips thick and bleeding, his breath coming in deep shuddering gasps.

Then Jim raised his bloody face to regard the circle of silent men gathered about him.

"What Indian squaw I see at night is my own business," he said hoarsely. "Does anyone else doubt that?"

Great, lovable Jim Wade! Sick and hurt as he was, propped among the three of us, he could still speak the lie that meant sanctuary for Ellen and shabby disgrace for himself. And anything further Santee ever said about this night would be known for a lie; the timing, the very violence of Jim's word carried utter conviction.

There was a tightness in my throat as Tom helped me carry Jim back through the wrecked saloon and up the stairs to his room. His big body was slack, his steps dragged. We set him in the deep chair and he slumped back, and Tom and I exchanged the br͓ ͓fest of worried glances before Tom said, "I'll get the surgeon," and left.

Jim was a sight. He had some deep cuts on his face and one ear was half torn off, three knuckles of his left hand were mashed and one eye was closing. As soon as I had washed him I poured out a stiff shot of whiskey that he drank off, holding the glass in a hand that trembled so the tumbler beat a little tattoo on his teeth. After that he leaned forward, his elbows on his knees, his swollen hands drooping limply, his head hung. He did not talk, and neither did I, during the long wait until Tom arrived with the surgeon.

He was an untidy little man, garrulous and smelling of whiskey and medicines. He looked shrewdly at Jim and then grunted.

"I've just come from watching Dr. Merrill work on Mr. Paddock. I believe you came off the winner."

"He isn't dead?" Jim asked.

"No."

"That's a pity," Jim said mildly, implacably.

"He'll wish he was, before he's out of it," the Doctor said. He stopped rolling up his sleeves and began to tick off items on his fingers as he spoke. "A broken nose — oh, a beautifully broken nose. Six broken ribs, five teeth missing and severe concussions. Then I'm saving the best until the last. A compound fracture of the jaw."

Jim didn't even look up. The doctor glanced at me and I said, "See about his ear, Doctor."

It was a long session getting Jim patched up. Before the doctor was finished, just as he was bandaging Jim's hand, there was a knock on the door and Tom, answering it, came to attention. Major Corning walked into the room, nodded to us and came over to Jim. He said, "All right, Jim?" and Jim said yes, and the doctor finished his work as quickly as he could, and then left. Tom went with him.

Major Corning was sitting stiffly in the straight chair as the door closed. He relaxed and lighted a cigar, then crossed his legs carefully and regarded us both, his glance finally settling on Jim.

"Well, it looks as if you'd done it, Jim," he said finally.

"Not a very good job," Jim said through thick lips.

The Major ignored this. He went on in a kindly voice, "I have a very unpleasant duty to perform."

"I can guess," Jim said without looking at him.

"Well, it can't be helped and I can't play favorites." He cleared his throat. "I'll have to ask you to stay away from the garrison, Jim. I haven't the details of the fight, but I don't need them. You can be sure that Santee, if he lives, will see that pressure is brought on me to make you meet the deadline, or else evacuate your leases with troops. I'll stick to the promise I made you tonight when you came over, however, and risk a reprimand. Then there's Captain Ford, the agent."

Jim still didn't look at him. Major Corning uncrossed his legs and recrossed them, and it betrayed his uneasiness.

"A white man's relations with Indian women is none of my business until it's brought to my attention. You can be sure Captain Ford will bring it. Not only because it's routine, but because he has a personal dislike for the Canadian Cattle Company. I'm ordering you to stay away from the garrison now, Jim, to save myself the embarrassment of doing it more publicly a bit later."

"I know," Jim said, still not looking at him.

"Mind you," Major Corning said slowly, "I'm taking the confused word of some of my officers who heard you speak out there below the porch. They could have been mistaken. If you say so, I'll give you a chance to deny it." There was an eagerness in his fine face that made me look away.

"No, they heard right," Jim murmured stubbornly.

Major Corning could not hide the disappointment he felt. He said tonelessly, "Well, there's no accounting for the tastes of your friends." He rose and came over to Jim and held out his hand. Jim took it, looking up at him.

Major Corning said, "This is a pretty sorry end to a pleasant friendship, Jim. Officially, I mean. Unofficially, if I can ever help you, call on me."

"Thank you, sir," Jim said.

Major Corning wanted to say more. He only said, "Hell," feelingly, wrung Jim's hand and went out.

Mechanically, I picked up the washbowl and took it back to the washstand, and all the while I was thinking of Major Corning's edict, and what Jim's banishment would mean to him and to Ellen.

When I came back, Jim was absently stroking the bandage on his hand, staring at the rug.

"Jim."

He looked up slowly.

"If you can't come back here, you'd better see Ellen tonight."

His glance fell to the rug again. "I know. I saw her," he said listlessly. He came to his feet slowly and walked over to the bed. He turned his face to me, and shook his head.

"Doug's still stubborn." He tried his old smile and it didn't come off. "A man can make his own luck up to a point, Joey. I'm way past that point."

Nine

We didn't make the deadline, not by many long weeks, for we had an area bigger than Massachusetts to empty of cattle. Nor did Major Corning move us off. All that long fall, while the deep grass cured and the wild plum thickets turned red, while the cottonwoods stippled the creek bottoms with gaudy yellow and the great sandy bed of the Cimarron lay white with fine frost in the dawn sun, our great round-ups took place before the trek to the Cherokee Outlet. I freighted supplies to remote wild reaches of the lease, while the life in the trees drained back farther into the ground and the earth slowly donned the threadbare coat it wore in winter. I slept in buggies under the tarp that covered my wagon, and in the sod line camps that we were abandoning, and most of the time I was alone.

I seldom saw Jim, for he was north in the Outlet still working for more range. When I did see him on his occasional visits to one of the round-up camps, he was not the old Jim, but a gaunt-faced harried man with that pinched look about the eyes of too much work, too much defeat.

We never spoke of Ellen because nothing was changed and there was nothing more to say. Douglas Preftake wouldn't divorce her nor allow her to divorce him, and Jim wouldn't have her as Preftake's wife. A year ago when I was with them I could persuade myself it would work out so they would have each other. I could make myself think Jim Wade could do anything and that Ellen was too lovely and in love for things to turn out any way but happily. But I had lived to see things Jim Wade couldn't do, and the fact that Ellen loved him had not altered circumstances thus far. Jim and Ellen hadn't changed, but I had; and in changing I had discovered, perhaps too soon, that not all questions were answerable, that justice was not immutable and that the lives of real people, unlike the lives of people in my childhood stories, had little direction and were handled by an indifferent author. The real life stories had no logical beginnings; they lagged and stumbled and reversed their morals, and ended either too abruptly or not cleanly and decisively. Jim's and Ellen's story, for instance, might not end at all; it had remained half told these many months now, with no conclusion in sight.

I came to know a hundred faces and a dozen campfires and the cold loneliness of a solitary dawn. The first blizzard of squaw winter caught me driving a spring wagon filled with the last odds and ends taken from headquarters camp. I was driving at the drag end of one of our huge trail herds moving north. Although the early blizzard did not split our herd it was an omen the gloomy crew did not miss.

That storm was only the introduction. Time and again in the weeks of our slow progress to the new range, snow squalls bore down on us. Eleven other company trail herds, as big and unwieldy and helpless as our own, were making their way north to new range, fighting to get on the Outlet leases before winter broke in earnest.

Half a day deep into the Cherokee Outlet, another blizzard caught us. This time, we could not hold the cattle and had to turn them loose in the face of the storm while we made our way to our new headquarters camp. It was a big sod shack built into a clay dune, with a stable almost as big to the west, and it was as bleak and forlorn as our spirits. After the blizzard blew itself out, the crew went out to see what losses we had sustained. They returned with disheartening news, for the trail-weary herds had suffered.

We were seeing bitter proof of the arguments

we had laid before the President. Our cattle had been given no time to learn this new country, and when the blizzard struck they did not know where shelter was. They could only drift in the open, cold and miserable, until the storm blew itself out.

But even more pressing problems confronted us. Our horses were gaunted and we had to have grain. Too, none of our crew had been to a store or post since the cold weather set in, and they had to be clothed.

I was detailed to go to Caldwell for the corn and the clothes, and McCune told me to make the rounds of the other company camps to determine their needs. The three remaining line camps were gloomy affairs, too. The temporary crews had been turned off and the old crew, strange to this land, could only set about patiently acquiring a knowledge of its shelter and feed like the cattle they herded, and with little time to do it in.

Weeks ago, Jim had been at the last camp and gone, bound for Caldwell for feed for the horses and food for the men. I followed him, making my way from one winter line camp of the Cherokee Outlet ranches to another, once having to lay over two days for another storm.

I rode into Caldwell the day before Christmas, cold, dirty, unshaven and feeling as awed as a countryman over the sight of so many people and the Christmas bustle. At the office, the stove was going but Jim was not there, and I took the opportunity to go to the barber shop for a shave, haircut, bath and a change into clean clothes I bought.

Afterwards I returned to the office, pulled the big leather chair up behind the stove, and for the first time in months I sat back to do nothing and pity myself for the Christmas in prospect.

I was sitting that way when I heard someone slowly climb the outside stairs. The door opened and Jim came in, but not in the gusty way of old. He did not see me immediately, turning to shut the door behind him. Taking off his hat, he tramped slowly toward the desk. Under his worn buffalo coat, he seemed to move like a man tired to his very soul. The cold had raised the color into cheeks that were etched with new lines, and the skin of his face was stretched tighter to mould the stubborn muscles of his jaw.

When he saw my coat, he stopped and stared at it, and for a second I had the impression of a man whose patience was shaping into a dangerous thing that simmered and boiled behind the iron control he showed the world.

Then he turned and saw me behind the stove, and alarm crept into his eyes.

"What is it, Joey?" he asked quickly.

I came out of the chair, saying, "Nothing, Jim, nothing," and watched the thin fear die back into his eyes, and then he smiled and it was the old slow smile as he shook my hand.

He had been kept in town two weeks, dickering with one of the Outlet ranchers for a range on the Cimarron and Eagle Chief River that afforded more protection than ours did. This afternoon, he had ridden out alone — since Mr. Tressel had gone back to Texas — to the ranch to close negotiations, and found that the man had changed his mind. He listened to my story of the losses we had already sustained, and said nothing. When I told him why I had come, he said that corn and food were already being freighted out, but that he had forgotten about the crew needing clothes. Forgetting this seemed to distress him, and I could tell he was blaming himself for not having remembered it. Perhaps the old Jim Wade would not have forgotten, but on the other hand the old Jim Wade would not have remembered to send whiskey and cigars to his men, as Jim had remembered to do.

Not once did he mention Ellen, nor did I.

In late afternoon, he rose and reached for his coat, informing me that he was heading back for headquarters ranch immediately.

"But it's Christmas tomorrow, Jim," I protested. "You've earned a day's rest and a big dinner. Have it with me."

He shook his head briefly. "They don't like me in this town, Joey." He smiled very faintly, then, "I've got so I dodge in a back alley to smoke a cigar. If I met a creditor with one in my mouth, he'd think I was riggin' the books. I think I'll ride out."

"If they're losing part of their stake, have they stopped to think that you're losing all of yours?" I asked.

"A rockin'-chair rancher don't think, Joey." He put out his hand and said gravely, "Merry Christmas," and, aware of the irony of it, I wished him one in return, and he left.

Twenty minutes later, rifling through the desk, I found Jim's Christmas present to me. It had my name on it, along with a Christmas greeting card; he had forgotten to tell me about it.

I stood there in the lowering dusk with the present in my hand, and waited for the charity of the season to come to me, and it did not. I could forgive neither the fates that dogged Jim Wade, nor the people here who had driven him to choosing a lonely ride on Christmas rather than face the silent censure of their company.

I unwrapped the present, bound that I would not celebrate Christmas if Jim could not. It was a pipe and I put it in my pocket and went out to make the purchases for which I had come.

Lowell's Emporium was where I turned in, and I was immediately caught in the press of people. When I broke from them for a place at the counter I found myself in front of Mr. Lowell. He nodded pleasantly to me, and when it came my turn to be waited upon, he extended his soft hand to shake mine effusively and say in hearty voice,

"Well, young man, I can guess what you're in town for."

"Warm clothes," I said.

He looked blankly at me. "We've been expecting you." His smile had already faded and I felt a premonition of something unpleasant to come.

I, in turn, looked blank, and Mr. Lowell said, "You didn't know Elizabeth was home?"

"No, sir," I said. "I haven't got around to picking up my mail yet."

Mr. Lowell seemed eager to seize on this explanation, however. "You've turned into a mighty busy man, Joel. Well, it doesn't matter. Elizabeth wrote you that we're expecting you for Christmas dinner. Why don't you come over tonight and help her trim our tree?"

"Why, I'd like to, sir. How is Elizabeth?"

He winked slyly, and said, "See for yourself tonight son."

I forgot I had any business there, and stepped back to let someone else take my place at the counter. I was uneasy and embarrassed by Mr. Lowell's friendliness. Our last meeting, I remembered, had not come off so well. But beyond that, I was both surprised and ashamed that I had forgotten Elizabeth entirely. Her last letter, written months ago, had told me she was coming home for Christmas, and I had forgotten it.

Later, when I stopped by the post office and found that my mail, along with that of the rest of the crew, had been called for by Jim that morning, I concluded that a special providence had guided me into Lowell's Emporium. Otherwise, I would have offended the Lowells beyond any explaining. For, truth to tell, I was more than a little curious about Elizabeth, and it was clear enough that she was curious about me.

It had begun to snow at dark, and as I made my round of the stores in the early evening on my errands for the crew, the quiet pleasure of Christmas Eve was communicated to me. People I did not know wished me a Merry Christmas; the harness bells on the bobsled and buggy teams made a music all their own, and the falling snow muted the raw clang of the church bells. I realized that for more than a year now my waking hours had been filled with the business of the company or with the gray contemplation of Jim's and Ellen's troubles. Tonight and tomorrow I would forget them; I would be with people who cared nothing for them nor for the company.

At the Drover's House I got a quick supper in the dining room and then went up to my room. In the back of my mind was a notion that I would change to clothes fit for a social evening, the clothes I had worn when I first came to Caldwell. But the sight of a choker collar and white shirt and a tie filled me with a firm distaste; I would wear them tomorrow, and assume that tonight my new pants and shirt and my old boots and sheepskin and worn Stetson would suffice.

I tucked Elizabeth's present — a volume of Longfellow's Poems that I had bought only an hour ago — under my arm and went downstairs and through the lobby. A stage was unloading in front of the hotel, and I stood aside to let a woman pass into the lobby.

We saw each other at the same time, Ellen and I, and she gave a small cry of pleasure and put her arms around me and hugged me. Her face was cold against my cheek, and she held me tightly for a moment. Captain Preftake came in then, and when he saw me his sober face broke into a slow smile, and we shook hands while Ellen was still in my arms.

She backed off then and said gaily, almost feverishly, "Joey, Joey. What a Christmas present! What are you doing?"

"Looking at you, and you're cold," I said, and we all laughed.

The miserable ride in the cold stage had brought a color that stained her cheekbones and brightened her eyes, giving her a quality of feverish excitement. With her long beaver coat and matching toque, which sat so jauntily on her bright golden hair, she looked handsome and tall and proud — and I was half in love with her again, as I always was upon seeing her after a long absence. But she was different this time; her face smiled and her brown-black eyes did not, and she knew I saw it, and she talked to cover it up.

"How many months has it been, Joey? All during the fall, hasn't it? You look like a Texas cowboy now." There was more of it, friendly woman-talk and banter, and all the time Captain Preftake was regarding her soberly.

Ellen put her arm through mine. "You were going out, Joey. You can't. Aren't we spending Christmas Eve together?"

Before I could answer, Captain Preftake stepped aside for the shivering colored porter who came in with two big valises. Captain Preftake unbuttoned his greatcoat then and left us, walking toward the lobby desk and the register.

"I'm afraid I am spending it somewhere else," I said to her.

"No. You can't go tonight, Joey. We've got to visit with you."

I looked at the big clock above the lobby desk, and saw it was after eight. I said, "A little while, but I've really got to leave soon." I didn't want to leave; I wanted to talk to her, when only an hour ago I had been glad for the chance to forget her.

She squeezed my arm in thanks, and we walked over to the desk, where the register lay open. Captain Preftake, hat in one hand, a handkerchief with which he was wiping his mustache in the other, walked over to the dining room, peered inside, and then signalled a waitress.

Ellen and I paused by the desk, and she reached out and turned the register around and picked up the pen from the glass of shot on the desk. Dipping it in the inkwell, she poised it above Captain Preftake's signature, which read "Capt. and Mrs. Douglas Preftake." Then she drew a line through the "and Mrs." and below it she signed her own name. Glancing up at the clerk who was watching her she said, "I'd like a room to myself."

She did not look at me, and I tried to move away. She put a hand on my arm and, still not looking at me, said softly, strangely, "Stay by me, Joey."

Captain Preftake came up then, a bill of fare

in his hand, and held it out to her. "The dining room will close soon, Ellen. Why don't we order now, and it'll be ready when we get down?"

The clerk, at that moment, laid a room key on the desk beside the one already there. Captain Preftake looked briefly at it, at the clerk, and then at Ellen. "What's this?" he asked slowly.

"I don't think I want dinner, Douglas," Ellen said quietly.

Captain Preftake looked quizzically at the clerk, as if he had not heard Ellen. I wanted to turn away, but I stood there stubbornly, mindful of what Ellen had said to me and not understanding any of this, except that things were not right between them.

The clerk said defensively, "Mrs. Preftake asked for a room of her own, Captain."

I saw a slow embarrassment creeping into Captain Preftake's face. He said quietly, "All right. All right," and laid the bill of fare on the counter and forgot it.

Ellen put her hand through my arm again, as if she were afraid I would bolt. "Come up with us, Joey."

I made one last effort. I said, "Ellen, I've promised −"

"And you've promised me." Her hand tightened on my arm, and I somehow knew again that I was being used. I knew, too, that I would have to make an unpleasant scene if I were to break away, so I gave in.

The colored boy had preceded us up the stairs, and had Ellen's room's door open, the lamp lighted and the stove going by the time we went in. Captain Preftake paused in the doorway, looked around, and when the colored boy hurried out, he left the room and followed him.

As soon as he was gone Ellen said to me: "Joey, I don't want you to leave me."

"But, Ellen, I've got to go to the Lowells' tonight. Besides, you're tired, and we've got all day tomorrow."

"Joey, don't leave. Promise me you won't leave!"

She sat on the bed, her coat still on against the chill of the room, and looked at me almost beggingly. Her spurious gaiety was gone now, and the dead soberness in her face was almost frightening. Here, right now, was some kind of a crisis the nature of which I could not even guess at, but her face, from which the flush of cold had fled, told me it was real enough. I had never been much good at denying her anything, nor was I any better at it now.

"What's happened, Ellen?"

"Nothing, Joey. But something will."

The lamp was beginning to smoke and I went

214

over to the table and turned down the wick. Then I knelt in front of Ellen and pulled off her overshoes. I looked up at her and surprised her watching me closely, with a kind of impersonal, almost cold speculation in her eyes. She smiled tiredly then and said, "Just this once, Joey," and I knew that whatever was coming I was going to be a part of it.

Captain Preftake entered then. He had left his greatcoat in his room and was rubbing his hands briskly as he came in. It was a natural, homely act, and I sensed he was doing it because he too was uncomfortable and uncertain of what was happening, and wanted to hide his uneasiness.

Ellen rose then and went over to the door and shut it, while I answered Captain Preftake's questions about our new leases on the Outlet. But my voice got vague, and my talk pointless; both of us were watching the purposeful movements of Ellen, and my talk finally faded and ceased.

She had taken off her coat and put it on the bed. The hem of her dark green cashmere dress was turned up, revealing her petticoat, but if she saw it she didn't care. She came into the middle of the room, facing Doug at the stove. Besides silencing me, her manner conveyed a subtle challenge to him; his face settled into stubbornness.

"Doug, I want to finish something now."

He sighed, and said patiently, "Ellen, I'm hungry and you're tired and Joel was going somewhere. Won't it keep till later?"

"No."

He reached in a pocket for his cigar case and said resignedly, "All right."

Ellen said, "You have thought all along I was coming up here to go away with Jim, haven't you, Doug?"

"You said you were."

"I lied to you. That's not why I came. I just lied to you. If you knew the real reason you would have stopped me."

Captain Preftake kept right on with the business of taking out a cheroot, closing the case and putting it back in the pocket of his tunic, but he was regarding her closely.

"I've come up here to get a divorce from you, Doug," Ellen said.

Captain Preftake said wearily, patiently, "Ellen, we've gone through all this before. I won't give you a divorce."

"Yes you will, Doug. You will because I'm going to trick you." She looked at me, an excitement and determination in her eyes. "Joey, this is dirty and mean and selfish, but I'm past caring about it."

I knew then I didn't belong here, and I rose and said, "Ellen, I've really got to go."

216

She was looking at Captain Preftake again, her eyes bright with something close to anger, but it was to me she spoke "You can't, Joey. You see, I've written a lawyer here. I know what I have to do. From now on I can't be alone with Doug."

I said resentfully, "This is why you wouldn't let me leave?"

Still, she didn't look at me. "Yes. I'm glad it was you, Joey, but if it hadn't been you it would have been anybody. I won't see Doug alone any more."

I understood, suddenly, that cold and calculating look I had surprised on her face minutes ago. She had been speculating on just how much help she could count on from me, and the thought of it shocked and angered me. It came to me just as suddenly then that maybe this duplicity was the measure of her desperation. I sank back on the bed, not liking this new and hard Ellen, even while knowing that she was fighting her woman's fight for Jim Wade.

I think her bland admission of trickery angered Captain Preftake, as it angered me. He said sharply, "I don't know anything about divorce, Ellen, but I do know there has to be a reason. What reason have I given you?"

"None, really. But I'll say to my lawyer that you were unfaithful to me, and he'll go ahead with that."

"You know that isn't true," Preftake said mildly.

"Of course it isn't. But I'll say it is."

Preftake looked at me, and his expression was one of bafflement and exasperation. He said something then that, in its flash of bitterness and irony, surprised me. "This is female logic, Joel."

His angry gaze shuttled back to Ellen, and he said patiently, in a tone a teacher might have used to a very small child, "When you go into court, Ellen, the burden of proof will rest upon you and your lawyer. You haven't any proof. You've just said so. Your case is lost before you start it, so why start it?"

"Ah," Ellen said softly. "Once I get into court I will announce that *I've* been unfaithful to *you*."

Preftake said sharply, "Ellen!"

"I haven't been, of course," Ellen went on calmly, "but that won't stop me from saying I have."

Captain Preftake, like myself, was staring at Ellen as if she were speaking in a language unknown to us.

He raised his hand to throw away his cigar, looked about him for some place to put it, and not finding one, held it. There was no reasonableness in his voice now. "You're talking like a feather-headed fool, Ellen," he said drily. "I can give you a dozen reasons you can't do that."

"None I don't know already."

"Do you think a judge will be mocked in that manner? You will be fined, and your lawyer punished."

"My lawyer won't know I'm going to do it."

"I'll tell him."

"I've thought of that. I've written him not to be surprised if you come to him with preposterous stories."

Captain Preftake was silent a moment, but he was angry still. "You'll be fined, maybe imprisoned."

Ellen said swiftly, "I haven't any money. I wouldn't mind prison, since I'm used to it."

Now Captain Preftake dropped his cigar on the ash apron under the stove and came over to hear. "Ellen, will you stop talking this nonsense? When you go through with it, and your divorce is denied, what will it have got you?"

Ellen said unsmilingly, "I thought you'd come to that. It will get me disgraced in public, Douglas. I will be smeared with all the slime I can make up, for a whole courtroom to hear. I will confess I am an adulteress — for all of them to hear."

It was I who cried out this time, "Ellen!" and I could not help it. The thing she was planning and the fact that she would confess it was

219

somehow shameful. I looked at Captain Preftake, and he was regarding her with sudden wonder and pity in his face. Ellen watched him with a hard and angry triumph.

Neither of them spoke for a full half minute, and then Ellen said, "You couldn't bear that, Doug. No man with pride could. And rather than have it mock you the rest of your life, I think you'll divorce me."

Still Captain Preftake said nothing; only an expression of pity was in his face.

Then I remembered what Ellen had said, and I, too, felt a pity for her. "Ellen, it won't work," I said quietly.

She turned her head to look at me, and I went on, "I've been reading law off and on for two years. I don't know much law, but I know your scheme won't work."

She didn't say anything; her face was set stubbornly, however.

"You'd have to live in Kansas a year before you could bring suit."

"I know that," she said quietly. "I'm prepared to. Is that what you mean?"

"No. You see your case won't be tried in court, with a crowd listening. The judge will try it in his chambers, and only he and the court reporter and you and Douglas and your lawyers will be there. And your witnesses — if you can buy any." I paused. "You'll be thought a fool woman, Ellen, by everyone there. But if your false confessions ever get outside the judge's chambers you will have to carry them yourself. Those men won't."

As I finished I saw a fathomless bitterness in her eyes. She looked steadily at me and said softly, "Is that true, Joel? You aren't lying to me?"

"I'm not lying."

She folded her hands in front of her and turned and walked over to the black window that looked out onto the street of Christmas Eve.

The room was so quiet that I could hear the steady draft of the stove, and I glanced over at Captain Preftake. He was watching Ellen with a sadness in his eyes that made me turn my gaze away. I stood up, hat in hand, feeling a guilt that I should not have felt. I had saved Ellen a disappointment which would have been keener than that which she was experiencing now. The fact she had staked everything on a scheme so frail, so sordid, so ridiculous told me that misery had been with her all these months. Truly, she was desperate.

I said, "I'm sorry, Ellen. Good night."

She turned slowly from the window and her gaze settled on Captain Preftake.

"I failed this time, Doug, but I won't give up. I'll never give up, not if I'm old and ugly and my hair is gray when I go to Jim."

I went across to the door and stepped out. Captain Preftake followed me, closing the door gently. We walked down the hall together a few steps, and then he put a hand on my arm and halted me.

I faced him, and we looked in each other's eyes. There was a hurt in his. "What have I done to her, Joey? Will you tell me?"

What was there I could tell him? That while he was a good and decent man and had made Ellen a fine husband, he must give Ellen up because she and Jim wanted him to? Or that because his whole world had risen against him through no fault of his own, he must submit to the blind idiocy of luck instead of fight for what he loved?

"Nothing," I said miserably. "I don't know. It's what happens to people, and they can't help it."

I left him standing there in the corridor and went down into the lobby. It was almost deserted, and I looked at the clock.

It said ten minutes after eleven. My evening with Elizabeth was gone, and I could not see her at this hour. I found I did not even want to, for Christmas Eve is a time of merriment and gladness, and I felt neither merry nor glad. I carried my book of Longfellow's Poems back to my room and went to bed.

* * *

I arrived at the Lowell's neat white house, with its carefully shovelled walk, a little past noon, dressed neatly and uncomfortably; and I was miserable. I had spent a sleepless night thinking of Ellen, and in the dark hours of morning I had come to a conclusion that by now was absolute conviction: this thing was destroying the three of them. Jim was breaking under it, losing his sharpness and his humor; Ellen had lost all happiness and had stooped to a cheap and stupid trick unworthy of her; and Captain Preftake, guilty only of being Ellen's husband was tormented and bewildered.

The day was still and gray and when I knocked on the door I tried to compose my face so that it would not reflect my low spirits. Too, I was worried, but not very much, about the reception I would get in the light of my nonappearance last night.

But when the door was opened by Mr. Lowell, my doubts on that score were dispelled.

"Merry Christmas, Joel, my boy!" he cried and shook my hand, pulling me into the house. The smell of cooking turkey and stuffing and mince pie and cake made my stomach coil with sudden hunger.

Mrs. Lowell and Elizabeth were waiting in the front room, and the first thing I noticed was that while Mrs. Lowell's long, stern face was flushed from the heat of the stove, Elizabeth's was not. The second thing I noticed was that Elizabeth talked with the eastern accent of her parents now, though she had been born in Illinois and grew up in Kansas. And the third thing I noticed, with slow shock to myself, was that the hair I had thought so golden was really straw-colored and ordinary, the skin I had thought so white was really sallow, and the mouth I had thought so full of character was really prim. I understood immediately the reason for Mr. Lowell's effusiveness, his forgiveness and his insistence that I spend this day with them: His daughter would be difficult to marry off, and I was a bet not to be overlooked.

I presented my gift and apologized for my absence last night, telling them frankly that old friends I had not seen in months kept me until the hour was too late for me to come here.

Elizabeth laughed nervously and said, "What a relief, Joel. Father forgot when he invited you that I wouldn't be at home Christmas Eve." She unwrapped my present and exclaimed, "How lovely! The binding is so much prettier than the one on my old Longfellow."

Having scored on me twice with what I was certain were two untruths, she and her mother retired to the kitchen and I was left with Mr. Lowell. He settled down in the only comfortable chair, remarked about the weather, and then asked me blandly about the affairs of the company. Christmas itself, the review of the presents, all the cheerful small talk of the day went by the boards; we had to talk business.

I gave a vaguely confident reply to his query, and was immediately asked to explain. It took less than five uncomfortable minutes for me to find out that Mr. Lowell, doubtless through the business men of the town, knew the state of our affairs almost as intimately as I did. With the imperturbable smugness of the second-guesser he reviewed our history, demanding to know what kind of business principles originally had allowed us to sell stock when there was no assurance our leases were valid, and no written guarantee of right of tenure. It had the characteristics of a monte game with fabulous stakes, he said, and he questioned the astuteness of the man who would promote this swindle. He meant Jim Wade, of course.

When Elizabeth came in to announce dinner, I was defending Jim Wade with a cold fury, and was not doing a job of it. Long ago I had told myself that Jim was a gambler, but I could not bear to hear him named so by a soft cautious man using hindsight for ammunition.

Elizabeth halted our conversation, and we silently filed in to dinner. Once we were all seated, Mr. Lowell took out just enough time to say a long grace, and then he was back on the subject of Jim Wade again, while he heaped my plate high with food. I shut his voice from my ears as best I could and watched Elizabeth to my left. She was listening carefully to her father at the head of the table. It came to me suddenly that I was watching the ghost of Mrs. Lowell as she was thirty years ago, and the thought held a cold interest for me. I looked at her hands, soft and round, and beneath the flesh of them I thought I could see the same thin ugly bones of her mother's hand which kept passing me food from my other side.

Minutes later, I was eating hungrily, deep in this morbid game of comparison, when I became aware of Elizabeth watching me curiously and, at the same time, of silence. They were all looking at me expectantly, as if waiting for me to answer a question.

I took a drink of water and said, "I'm afraid I didn't get your question, sir."

"I asked you how any reasonable man could protest President Cleveland's evacuation order in the light of these facts."

"What facts, sir?"

He looked annoyed. "The facts I've just presented."

"Plenty of them did protest."

"And he gave them little comfort."

"He did — after admitting they were right."

He smiled tolerantly. "I doubt that."

"Then inform yourself, sir," I said, shortly. There was a moment of surprised silence, and then Mrs. Lowell stepped into the breach and changed the subject. I looked down at my plate, aware that I had been rude and not caring much. A man who would invite you to his house and then slander your friends was deserving of insolence.

Mrs. Lowell was discussing the church sermon this morning in derogatory terms, comparing it with the sermons that the Lowells had heard in Boston from the mouth of the Reverend Henry Ward Beecher. I was listening dutifully, still angry with Mr. Lowell, when Mrs. Lowell turned to me and asked, "You've never had the privilege of hearing Reverend Beecher, have you, Joel?"

Her tone was just patronizing enough to stir my malice, and I asked with a quiet innocence, "Isn't he the gentleman of the cloth who defended himself so ably in that famous lawsuit for adultery?"

Mrs. Lowell gave a quick cough and looked at her husband, and I could see her blushing.

"That is filthy slander!" This came from Elizabeth with such passion that I turned to her and saw her face was thin and waspish with anger. My malice was further stirred, and I said,

"But I didn't accuse him of adultery, Elizabeth. Another man did."

Mr. Lowell said firmly, "Please, Elizabeth, that's not a subject we'll discuss in this company."

Elizabeth was still looking at me, still angry. "All right, father," she said sweetly, "but I didn't introduce the subject. Joel did. Perhaps because he's familiar with it."

"Adultery?" I asked in amazement.

"Joel! Elizabeth!" Mr. Lowell said sharply.

Elizabeth blushed furiously, but she went on in her sharp voice, "You know very well what I'm talking about, Joel! Jim Wade! It's common talk!"

I put down my fork, feeling a surge of wrath mounting in me. "What is common talk?"

"Elizabeth!" Mrs. Lowell said angrily.

But Elizabeth was heedless. "Everyone knows about the fight he had in Reno over that Indian squaw! And everyone knows he was protecting another woman!"

"What woman?" I asked in a low voice.

"Ask Jim Wade! You know him so well!"

I looked from Elizabeth to Mr. Lowell, and I could see the same smug, half-fearful accusation on his face that was on Mrs. Lowell's face when I looked at her. I knew then that I did not belong with these people, and it was my utter disgust and anger that I blame for what followed.

I rose from my chair, put my napkin beside my plate and said in cold and mocking fury, " 'Good will toward men.' Maybe you're having that for dessert, Mrs. Lowell, but I won't wait. Thank you, and good day."

I tramped past Elizabeth's chair and Mr. Lowell rose and put his hand on my arm. I shook it off, and got my hat and coat and stepped outside and went down the walk.

I heard the door open and I heard Elizabeth call, "Joel! Joel!" only it was in a restrained voice that was almost a hiss, so that the neighbors would not hear her.

I did not even look around. That walk back to the hotel was hurried and purposeful. I wanted to get out of Caldwell and never see it again, and my anger never left me. And the thought that kept my fury alive was that the hell Jim and Ellen had gone through amounted only to this, that it was the subject for the vindictive gossip of these "good people."

I left Caldwell within half an hour.

It was after midnight when I rode into our closest line shack on the edge of the lease and turned my horse into the corral and fed him some of the new corn.

Inside the shack I struck a match and looked around me before I went over to the table where a candle stub was roosting on a can lid. There was nobody here, I thought, and I supposed that, after the custom of the country, our men had ridden over to the neighboring ranches to spend Christmas.

I had one boot off when I heard a deep sigh from one of the bunks across the way. Taking the candle, I went over to see who it was, and there was Jim asleep, his face turned toward the wall.

A sleeping man looks lonely to begin with, and when I realized that Jim had probably spent Christmas Day in this shack by himself, I felt a strange discouragement. This could never have happened to the Jim Wade I first knew; either he would have had half the country crowded in here for a barbecued beef, or he would have had his choice of half a hundred invitations in Caldwell.

I took to my blankets without waking him.

He was up ahead of me in the morning, and his thin whistle roused me. Lying awake for a half minute in my blankets, I knew I was not going to tell him about seeing Ellen and Captain Preftake Christmas Eve, nor about my dinner at the Lowells'.

When I came out of the bunk he said, "How was the dinner, Joey?"

"What dinner?" I asked suspiciously. He was warming some steaks at the stove, and he glanced over at me.

"Why, that Christmas dinner with the Lowells."

"How did you know I had dinner there?" I demanded.

He grinned faintly. "Old man Lowell had a boy on every corner in Caldwell lookin' for you. He told me to tell you, and I forgot."

I said shortly, "It was all right," and leaned over to pull on my boots.

When I looked up at him, he was watching me curiously, frowning. "Joey, you been eatin' off tin plates too long. You're gettin' shy of a white shirt and a girl."

"If you mean that girl, I am," I said firmly. "How about a tin plate, then, and some food?"

All that morning, the last before we reached the mean sod shack among the clay dunes that was our headquarters, we watched the winter sky build up behind us, layer on layer of slate-colored clouds that piled up above the low ceiling of the prairie. The air was mild, still as standing water, charged with a breathless expectancy that made our horses uneasy. A little after noon it began to snow gently, the flakes falling as straight as if they were leaded. In mid-afternoon, they took on a slant to the south, and inside of a half hour, the blizzard was on us. It came smoking out of the north, dragging a fathomless darkness with it that rode with snowflakes as small and sharp and hard as glass particles.

Jim and I were riding abreast. When the full

fury of the wind hit me, I doubled forward over the saddle horn and felt my horse stumble to keep his feet and then when I shoved myself up I was looking at a streaking blurred world that ended two feet from my face. I tried to rein in, but my horse could not stop; he was being propelled by the same iron fury at his back that was trying to pry me out of the saddle. In panic, I reined him toward the right, where I had last seen Jim, and presently our two horses collided gently and kept walking shoulder to shoulder. I tried to see Jim, but could make out only an indistinct blur beside me. I felt his hand on my leg and then on my arm and I fumbled for it, shouting that I was all right. I felt for his hand and what I found was the end of his lariat, the hondo. He would not give it up, but fumbled around until he had found the horn of my saddle and slipped the rope over it. Then he found my reins and dragged a foot of them through my gloves before his hand vanished, and I knew that he was trying to tell me to give my horse free rein.

Then he disappeared ahead of me, and I grabbed at the horn. The few feet of rope I could see swung in a slow quarter circle until it vanished past the neck of the horse, and I knew Jim was ahead.

It was like being submerged in a brawling swift-moving stream, and I do not know how long, how many hours I just sat in the saddle, my eyes shut, my hands locked over the horn to keep Jim's rope there, and listened to the wicked sustained scream of that wind. Presently, we changed our course, and now the wind caught us quartering, and I could feel my horse fighting across it, his head half turned away from the wind's force.

My face was utterly stiff, my right cheek burning with a wicked pinpoint pain that was frost burning into the flesh, and I tried to hide it in the collar of my sheepskin. Head buried, my hands locked on the horn in that dark, the calves of my legs sheathed with a cold that was driving into the bone, it seemed as if I suffered uncounted hours. We plowed through drifts so deep I felt my feet plowing furrows in the wind-packed snow.

And then, sometime in the night, the wind seemed to let up abruptly and my horse stopped. I tried to rowel him on, but he would not move. I felt for the rope, and it was slack, drooping toward the ground. Jim had dropped it. In panic I swung off, keeping hold of the rope and within two stumbling steps I had bumped into Jim. He grabbed my arm roughly and hauled me toward him and suddenly there was an utter lull in the wind's cry and I saw a building beside me.

In a moment a match flared, and I saw we

were in the headquarters stable. Jim's eyelashes and eyebrows were white with frost, and his coat collar that cut across his face was white too.

"You all right?" he said. He yelled it, forgetting that he was not talking against the wind now.

I nodded. Jim found the lantern and we brought our two ponies in among the others there. Rubbing them down and graining them gave us enough exercise to warm us up.

Afterwards, Jim took our two lariats and two more from saddles in the stable, tied them together, then said, "All you got to do, Joey, is follow this. I'll tie one end to the door hasp and trail it to the house."

"Do you want the lantern?" I asked, as he tied one end of the rope to the doorframe.

He only moved his head in negation and I put a hand on his arm. "Jim, what'll this do to the cattle?'

He only shrugged, and then disappeared into the night. I could hear him stumbling alongside the wall to the bank of the dune that the shack was dug into, and then he left the stable wall and I waited by the rope. After an interminable time, I felt it tighten and then quiver. I blew the lantern out and lunged into the night. The sweep of the wind, even behind the clay dune, wrenched loose my grip on the rope and threw me onto the ground and tried to roll me over. I took my bearings and crawled the ten feet back into the stable and then started again, this time wrapping my arms around the rope.

Hugging the rope tightly, I drove my feet into the snow and inched my way toward the cabin, which was only some hundred feet away and utterly invisible. Head down I rammed into something with a violence that hurt, and then I was yanked through the big drift that banked the door.

McCune and Jim steadied me, and I raised my head out of my coat collar to find myself in the shack, breathing the hot-smelling air of the room.

Three of the crew beside McCune were here, and they were quiet all through the long evening, except to ask Jim how bad it was. All of us, with that blizzard wind clawing at the eaves and piling a fine sift of snow on the window sills and under the door, were thinking of the cattle. All we could hope for now was that it would blow itself out shortly and give us a chance to aid the cattle while there was still time. Luckily McCune, in our absence, had ordered riders in all the line camps to shove the cattle up to the north boundary. They had the whole deep width of the lease in which to drift before the blizzard. How long would it last?

I went to bed with the fitful muffled screaming of the wind in my ears and the last thing I heard was its mauling at the windows and the door as it seemed to shake the very house.

I woke up to it, too, and lying there in the bunk before I got up it seemed to me that we were in some great jungle, the only thing between us and the ravening beast of the storm the flimsy doors of the shack.

I don't know whether or not Jim slept that night. But I only needed to look at him at breakfast that morning to know that the thing we most feared, the thing that could destroy us, was here now. In the middle of breakfast Jim shoved his plate aside and stood up.

McCune, desperation in his face, said, "What do you want us to do, Jim?"

"That south fence has got to be cut to let those cattle drift," Jim said grimly. "I'm not askin' any man to go out in this, but I've got to do what I can."

One of the crew stood up and said bitterly, "By God, I'm not goin' to sit around here and let good beef die. I'm goin', Jim."

All of us were going. The profane cow-puncher had expressed what all of us felt. Even if we didn't succeed, we would know we had tried.

We put on all the clothes we could find, even taking the blankets from the bunks, cutting holes in them and slipping them over our heads, poncho fashion. We wrapped our feet in tow-sacking, and tied bandannas around our ears. We found enough files and wire cutters to go around, and Jim advised us all to carry guns and ammunition, a day's bait of corn for our horses and some biscuits for ourselves.

After that, we made the trip to the stables, one by one. Each man as he passed the corner of the house out into the clean sweep of the white wind, lost his feet and hung grimly to the rope until he regained them. It was a driving whirlpool outside now, and the great breath of the wind as it veered ate some drifts to nothing and built others up under our very eyes.

Once in the stable and our mounts saddled we pooled our information as to where shelter could be found when we reached the fence. After that, roughly dividing a long stretch of the fence between us, we set out.

Jim and I kept together. The visibility was better now than it had been yesterday, so that we did not need the rope. All we could do was sit in our saddles, keeping the horses close together, and let the wind at our backs coast us to the line fence far to the south.

I reckoned we had been riding two hours when the land fell away and we rode a deep cut that lay lengthwise to the wind. And there, riding up on top of them, we came to a bunch of cattle. Heads down, blind with cold and fear, they slogged woodenly on with the wind at their backs.

Jim yelled something to me and beckoned me to the right, and then he put his horse out into the drifts at the left. We rode around the slowly moving herd, and once at the head, we tried to turn them into the little offshoot canyons lying crossways to the wind where there would be shelter. Time and again we tried to turn them, throwing our horses into the leaders and letting off our guns in their faces. But they were crazed with cold and weariness. They meant to keep that wind at their backs until it died or they died.

I saw but couldn't hear Jim cursing as he pulled his horse away and signalled me to let them drift. Riding onward, we came to other scattered herds, all slogging south and indifferent both to our presence and to our furious efforts to turn them into the broken lands that lay on either side.

It was here that I lost Jim. I had come to rely on his looming out of the swirling blizzard, and I worked blindly trying to turn the leaders, waiting for him to come alongside and pull me away. But when, after minutes had passed, he did not come, I looked around. I could see nothing except sullen cattle. All I could do was ride alongside the leader waiting for Jim to follow the herd to its head.

An hour later, however, I knew we were separated. I could not turn back after him, for my horse would not have lasted two hours bucking that blizzard. All I could do was drift until I reached the fence and then cut it. We could find each other down there.

I knew when I came to the fence because I could hear the cattle bawling above the wail of the blizzard. Hundreds of them, bunched in a coulee against the fence, were fighting and trampling one another and shoving and gouging in their panic effort to get under way again.

I knew that if I succeeded in climbing the fence and cutting it from the other side I would be trampled in the ensuing stampede. I cut the fence on either side of the swale, trusting the overflow of the oncoming herds to find the break and go through.

After that, I followed the fence blindly, cutting it in every low place where the cattle were most apt to approach it. And time and again I saw small herds, their numbers swelling hourly, bawling and fighting and trampling each other in their mad effort to get on.

It was in one of these small swales, almost at dark, that I put my horse into the drift burying the fence, fumbled for and found the top wire, then dismounted and tied the reins to it. After floundering along in the drifts to the center of the swale I began to dig away the snow to get at the bottom wire. I was working with numbed hands, wondering how far the shelter was that the crew had told me about, when I felt the ground tremble under me. I wheeled and saw through the smoking wind that a mass of cattle was pouring into the swale like a great tidal wave. When they struck the deep drifts, the leaders sank and the others, fighting to crawl over their backs, trampled them down. They, in turn, bogged down in the drifts and were trampled themselves. Nothing short of annihilation could stop that march.

I judged the distance to my horse and knew I could not make it and for one brief instant I knew a raw, soul-curdling fear for my life.

In wild panic I cut the remaining wire and then lunged across the fence and fought my way through the drifts toward the rising ground beyond and to the right. I heard my horse scream but I did not even look back at him. Gagging for breath I lunged and fell and rose and lunged and fell again, holding that obscured height of land ahead of me as a goal.

Finally, when I had got out of the deepest drifts, I lifted my legs above the snow and ran like a madman, falling at last into a tangle of sagebrush on the slope, dead beat, unable to get up and waiting for the cattle to reach me.

They missed me by a scant ten feet, and I have never seen a more awesome sight in my life than their mad, blind march past me. Then they were gone in the curtain of snow, heading south. I went back to the fence, and my mind almost refused to believe what my eyes saw there. The crossing of that deep-drifted swale by the cattle was made literally on a floor of trampled steers, a hundred or so of them.

I ran over to where I had left my horse, fearful that he had been carried along with the cattle. He had not been that fortunate. Where I had left him there was only a great fast-spreading crimson blob of piled horse and cattle flesh. Bogged down in the drifts, his reins tied to the wire, he had served as the bottom step for the ladder of flesh that was built for the cattle to crawl on. The topmost steer, tangled in the wire and in the slippery mound of flesh, was alive and bawling in measured agonized bellows.

I found my gun and put a bullet through his head and finished off some others, and then in the awful howling solitude that engulfed me, I began to understand my plight. Afoot in this blizzard, not knowing where I was, unable to see twenty feet in any direction and darkness already coming, I was in a fair way to mingle my bones with the broken bodies of these cattle.

What I did then was compounded of instinct and panic and genius. My greatest fear was the cold, which was already chilling my sweat-soaked body.

Slogging over to the fence, I cut all the wires, and saw the pile of cattle flesh tilt and fall over. And then, my wire-cutters forgotten, I came back and started to dig in that pile.

Before complete darkness engulfed me, I had dug and hauled and shoved until I had a warm, blood-soaked pocket in that heap of bodies that I could crawl into. I took time to wolf down a half-dozen biscuits and then I crept into my bloody den. The warm bodies of the cattle, above and on three sides of me, would hold their body heat for hours and hours, I knew; and that body heat would keep me alive.

I lay with my head jammed against the hair of a steer's flank, my knees drawn tight against my chest so my feet were out of the wind. Every sudden move threatened to collapse this rubbery mass of flesh on me and engulf me, and I lay there, warm and awake, so that if the entrance to my cave drifted over and threatened to smother me, I could kick the drifts away. And I went to sleep, of course, with the proud thought in the back of my mind that I was still awake and would stay awake.

I was roused by the bitter cold and bright glare of the sun on snow that reached even into my cave. When I tried to move, I found my coat frozen to a bloody hide, but I managed to wrench it loose and back out of my cave.

Standing up, I was blinded for a moment. The day had dawned clear and clean, with not so much as a wisp of cloud in the deep far blue of the heavens. A savage, killing cold was on the land, the kind that stiffened my nostrils and reached clear to my throat and made me cough.

As I looked over my half acre of carnage, it was almost obscured by the steam from the still warm bodies of the cattle below. It lay like a brown smear over the floor of the swale.

I gathered all the sage and rabbit brush I could find, then cut a steak from one of the dead steers, built my fire, scorched the redness out of the meat, wolfed down my breakfast and the last of my biscuits, and then, considerably heartened, pondered what I was to do. My best bet was to travel the fence, keeping to the high land that was scoured clean of drifts by the wind, and eventually I was bound to meet one of our riders.

Accordingly, I set out traveling the fence line, and before I had gone a half mile I didn't need Jim Wade to tell me what the storm had done to us. In every swale, every coulee, with scarcely a break for the high land, our cattle lay in great windrows against the fence. Those still alive had survived only to have their frozen tails break off like icicles, their frozen hooves drop off. Not one, not dozens, but hundreds of these tortured cattle were standing on the stumps of the hoofless legs and lowing softly and pitifully in that bitter morning cold.

I used up all my shells putting them out of their misery. I cursed until there were tears in my eyes and murder in my heart. It was appalling beyond description — all this because Washington would not believe us when we said that for a steer to survive he had to have time to learn where his shelter was.

When my shells gave out and I knew that over the next rise, the next hundred rises, I would see this same suffering, I could not bear to look at it. I turned away from the fence and traveled parallel to it, out of sight and hearing of this suffering.

Our crew had done the best it knew how. Much of the fence was cut, and a small fraction of the cattle had drifted through the breaks, but it had not saved the majority of them. And it had not saved us.

It was almost noon when I heard shots to the southeast. I debated building a fire or making for the shot, and I chose the latter, fearful that a fire this far would not attract attention.

I cut back for the fence, and once more the shots came, closer this time. Picking the place where I thought I could intercept the rider coming west, I ran.

I came to the low bluff that sloped down to the fence. There, in the bright morning sun, was Jim. He had a rope around the head of a dead steer, and was helping his horse skid the steer aside. A dozen cattle were pulled out into the clean snow, and Jim was working with the steady sustained fury of a monomaniac.

"Jim!" I yelled.

He wheeled toward the sound of my voice, slowly raised his hand, and then sat down in the snow where he had been standing. When I reached him he was on his feet, his face flushed, breathing hard.

"I lost my horse in a stampede," I said lamely.

"You aren't hurt?"

"That's not my blood. I slept in a pile of dead cattle."

Jim slowly scrubbed his face with trembling hand, and for the first time I realized that these dozen cattle here, and I don't know how many dozen beyond, had been dragged away to see if I were buried beneath them.

Jim fixed his bright fevered gaze on me and then murmured, "Well, you're one thing that ain't dead, Joey."

"How bad is it, Jim?"

"It just couldn't be worse. A ninety percent loss, I reckon, if we're lucky." His glance raised to look at the still steaming mass of cattle sprawled against the fence. Beyond, three steers which had scaled the ladder of cattle flesh to cross the fence were standing in the cold sunlight, moaning.

When Jim's few remaining shells were exhausted, we turned back to headquarters ranch, riding double. I had already made up my mind that when we got to the shack tonight I would tell Jim I was through. Once before he had asked me to stay, and he would ask me again and I would refuse this time. For Jim, along with the company, was ruined. When he came out of this, it would be with only the clothes on his back, and he would probably ride back into Texas and there fade into obscurity. I was certain of this last, because I knew he didn't care. He'd lost Ellen, and he'd lost the company, and they were the only two things he really cared about. There is no sadder thing in this world than to see a king deposed, and I had seen one. There was only one thing for me to do then and that was to go quietly, for I could not help Jim, only burden him. Nor could I help Ellen and Douglas Preftake.

We came into headquarters ranch when early dark was almost on us. There was enough light left, however, for me to see the tracks of a buggy in the snow before the house. I looked off toward the stables, and saw the top buggy, its shafts propped up, backed into a drift. Our creditors, I supposed, had come to confirm the extent of the blizzard's disaster, and I said bitterly, "I suppose the buzzards have to gather some time."

"Now or later, what's the difference?" Jim answered quietly.

We put up our horse and grained him, and started back toward the shack. I knew Jim was in for a gloomy session of recrimination and whining from the men waiting inside, and I wished savagely that my last job for him might be to accept it myself and spare him.

Jim went in first, pushing the door wide and stooping a little for the low lintel. He halted so abruptly, then, that I pushed into him. I looked where he was looking, and saw Ellen rise from the bunk in the dusk of the hot shack.

Jim didn't speak. He walked into the room. A man, the hostler from the livery stable, came out of a chair against the wall and said, "Howdy, boys," and when nobody answered him he brushed past me and went out.

Ellen came toward Jim, and Jim said, almost harshly, "Why make it worse, Ellen?"

Ellen said, "Doug is tired of living with a fool woman, Jim. That's what I am without you." She paused. "He's promised to give me a divorce."

Jim didn't move, nor did Ellen.

I went out, then, closing the door behind me. I went out into the snow and saw the evening

247

star bright-hard and glittering, and I knew the cold was not over yet. The hostler was standing over by the stable, patiently stamping his feet in the snow, and I started toward him.

It took me some seconds to realize I was whistling. When I came up to the hostler he ceased his stamping and said, "How soon you figure she'll want to go back?"

I said, "Oh, fifty or sixty years," and when he looked disgusted at what he thought was a poor joke, I laughed.

THORNDIKE-MAGNA hopes you have
enjoyed this Large Print book. All
our Large Print titles are designed
for easiest reading, and all our
books are made to last. Other
Thorndike Press or Magna Print
books are available at your library,
through selected bookstores, or
directly from the publishers. For
more information about current
and upcoming titles, please mail
your name and address to:

THORNDIKE PRESS
P. O. Box 159
THORNDIKE, MAINE 04986

or in the United Kingdom:

MAGNA PRINT BOOKS
LONG PRESTON NEAR SKIPTON
NORTH YORKSHIRE,
ENGLAND BD23 4ND

There is no obligation, of course.